MW01674986

A Disputed Inheritance

The Story of a Cornish family. Second Edition.

SALZWASSER
VERLAG

Thomas Hood

A Disputed Inheritance

The Story of a Cornish family. Second Edition.

Reprint of the original, first published in 1863.

1st Edition 2022 | ISBN: 978-3-37500-726-3

Verlag (Publisher): Salzwasser Verlag GmbH, Zeilweg 44, 60439 Frankfurt, Deutschland
Vertretungsberechtigt (Authorized to represent): E. Roepke, Zeilweg 44, 60439 Frankfurt, Deutschland
Druck (Print): Books on Demand GmbH, In de Tarpen 42, 22848 Norderstedt, Deutschland

A DISPUTED INHERITANCE.

A DISPUTED INHERITANCE.

The Story of a Cornish Family.

BY THOMAS HOOD.

SECOND EDITION.

LONDON:

1863.

Dedication.

TO THE RIGHT HONOURABLE

LORD VISCOUNT TORRINGTON

THIS VOLUME IS INSCRIBED,

IN GRATITUDE FOR MANY KINDNESSES,

BY THE AUTHOR,

THOMAS HOOD.

PREFACE.

A portion of the following story appeared under another title in "Saturday Night." It was written some three years ago, when I was fresh from the scenery of the beautiful county to which it relates. I venture to hope it will receive a not unkindly welcome at the hands of the public. Should it do so, I shall be encouraged to attempt a more ambitious story another time.

T. H.

A DISPUTED INHERITANCE.

The Story of a Cornish Family.

CHAPTER I.

CHIEFLY FAMILY-HISTORICAL.

THE Tresellans of Tresellan were among the oldest families of England. They were at Hastings, and goodness knows how many other battles for the sovereignty before that. There was a crusading escalop to be seen in their coat armour, in days when the greatest Turnstile in all Lincoln's Inn Fields would not have dared to find one a scutcheon of arms for three and sixpence.

The particular knight who picked up the shell on the shores of Palestine reclined in effigy, with crossed legs, beside his lady in the church of St. Tude, a bowshot from Tresellan. The church of St. Tude (whoever he or she might be), was the parish church of what was, by courtesy, called the town of Polvadnick. Yet why not a town, when its two members, about the time of my story, sat in Walpole's parliament, and probably pocketed his bribes?

For the Tresellans I am going to talk about lived in the reign of his Protestant majesty George the Second, and prayed, I hope, very devoutly, in St. Tude's edifice every Sunday, to be defended from the creed of their benighted ancestors, and the wooden shoes of their lively neighbours across the Channel.

The Defender of the Faith protected us English from the Pope's iron rule, and the French king's aldern sabots, sitting throned at St. James's Palace on the shady side of Pall Mall. Along those broad flags, idle M.P.'s did not then loiter, nor industrious Government clerks hurry. But mall was played in the park hard by, and I have no doubt that the stout little gentleman, who did us the honour to rule our destinies, looked on, and presided at the game, if he did not play. They were strange times, my masters! They used to have little parties in St. James's Palace then. They positively fiddled and danced there. Just imagine what that tall grenadier sentry would do to me if he caught me tuning my violin within those gloomy precincts now-a-days! He would hand me over incontinently to those other scarlet giants (who spend their time and money on brandy balls and peppermint drops vended close at hand), by them to be thrust into the guard-room.

And oh! how they gambled in the palace then, and lost and won more guineas than I ever had to count every night of their lives, and that too in an atmosphere not kept over-refined by the language. For George was blunt, and spent no time in digging in the Trenches of the period for the synonym of spade; and the court, copying him, caricatured him as might be expected. Ah! well, if I cannot play my modest first fiddle under that smoky old clock tower for fear of that grenadier I give up any lurking desire to do so gladly, while I remember how much better our palace is now than it was when such scrapings and elbow shakings were allowable.

The goddess of card-built fortune has quitted that building to loiter, it may be in the neighbourhood—behind iron doors—and perchance in those grand club-houses—

> "Extrema per illos
> Justitia (?) excedens terris vestigia fecit."

But the palace has a better odour than of card parties, and of the violet powder of those fair creatures that hovered around the sentimental little king, who declined in such touching words to take a second wife. There is better music than that of fiddles when the regimental bands play enchantingly with stirring strains as pretty nursemaids listen, smiled on by downy-lipped cornets.

In the time of George, the town of Polvadnick did not in reality take up much more room than an ordinary village. And for obvious reasons. The river Perl, rising somewhere on a moor, covered with granite boulders, and wandering down through oak copses and green pasture land, with ever and anon a sandy reach or a fussy miniature cataract, flowed into the sea with a high precipitous headland (whereon stood Tresellan) on its right, and leaving on its left a small amphitheatre of shore above the tide-line. On this, which a modern factory would not find roomy enough, the town of Polvadnick grew. Even Polvadnick found it not entirely adequate to all its requirements. Its gardens were pushed out of the town and up the steep sides of the hill in terraces until the "hanging pleasances," like those of Babylon, made a series of gigantic steps round the amphitheatre. The people of the town were of the tribe of fishers. Long black nets perpetually basked along the beach, and in winter the boats were often dry-docked in the streets, which had always an ancient and a fish-like smell.

In the season all the men went off to the whiting grounds in the little fleet of boats that for the rest of the year rocked in the bay, and then the women collected in the church and lit their lamps in the tower at night for a beacon to their sons and husbands far away at sea.

For St. Tude's stood right out on the shore, as if to order back the waves; though the fishermen, not relying only on the saint, had another defence in the shape of a stout sea wall, against encroaching Oceanus.

Gallant men were the Polvadnick fishers. Long before a section of orange-rind had suggested a life-boat to some thoughtful observer, these men had gone out in the dark night, when the wind shook every casement in Tresellan, and the wild foam ran up the steep face of the cliff and came hissing against the window panes, when the unwieldy ships, with their fatal hugging of the shore, had come crashing on some of the jagged Cornish reefs. I know, here, I shall be told about "wreckers." So there might have been wreckers westward, but there were none within reach of the strong arm of the Tresellans of Tresellan. And I will tell you why. In the reign of Elizabeth, when all men were emulating the voyages of Raleigh, Sir Jasper Tresellan of Tresellan had sailed in his own galleon to the Brazils. His crew was the flower of the Polvadnick fishers. For eight long years Tresellan had no lord, and his people began to talk of Sir Jasper as of one who was dead.

But it was not so. He and his crew had landed, and made their temporary settlement. There they left a handful well armed, while the remainder pierced into the interior in search of the gold region.

The history of the expedition is that of a hundred others. Decimated by famine, pestilence, and the crafty savage, only a few crawled back to the landing place—in fact not enough to man the great galleon, at once their only refuge and their direst care; for when the storms swept the coast they feared every moment, with a fear amounting to agony, to lose this last tie between their native land and them. At length their number was recruited by stragglers from other stations on the coast, and they began the weary journey home—weary, but oh! how welcome.

It was not till they were out of sight of land,

that they discovered their captain was a maniac. Poor Jasper, worn down with fever and aged with care, had become mad when he thought of return. They watched him tenderly, and save a few fierce, brief outbreaks now and then, he behaved with tolerable calmness. But when they sighted the north coast of Cornwall, and all hoped to land at the first haven, his wild fury broke out. "He would put in at the port he sailed from, he would sink his ship where she was launched." Many remembered his mad words afterwards. And so they toiled round the Land's End and the Lizard until they passed the Deadman's Head, and the little bay of Polvadnick lay before them. It was dusk but Jasper insisted on attempting the passage, although the tide would hardly serve. Whether absence had impaired his memory, or premature age dimmed his sight, or whether it were a voluntary act, as some judged from the words I have quoted, it is impossible now to determine; but certain it is the great galleon was impaled on the Sharphead Rocks, just in front of the town, in that calm evening, with scarcely a breath stirring. By the faint light of the stars just beginning to twinkle, and by the dim rays of the rising moon, the flotilla of wreckers' boats set out. They gathered around the doomed vessel, preparing for a rush. Sir Jasper ran out on the bowsprit.

"A Tresellan!" he cried. "Come, sea-dogs, and feed on your brothers. We sailed from Polvadnick eight years ago. A merry greeting to all!"

With these words and a wild laugh, the poor gentleman threw himself into the sea. The next day his body was washed ashore.

Of course, his speech altered the aspect of affairs. The wreckers immediately busied themselves in removing the crew, and many were the recognitions that took place, though more the inquiries never responded to, and the names called that no one was living to claim.

The next morning the galleon broke up, sooner than was anticipated, for the fishermen did not know what the influences of that strange foreign sea had been upon the old vessel.

From that time the Tresellans (Sir Jasper's younger brother succeeded him), never suffered the people of their town to wreck; but lordly were the rewards and kindly the welcomes that fell to the rescuers and the rescued when the sea was gnashing white on the Sharphead Rocks, and the distress guns booming and echoing up the valley of the Perl.

Sir Jasper's tomb in the church of St. Tude is within the chancel, beside the monumental brass of Sir Philip Tresellan, killed at Agincourt—

"On whose soule and on all Crysten soules Jhu habe mercy. Amen."

So runs the ancient legend. Opposite, is the mausoleum of Sir Geoffrey, cup-bearer to James I., whereon a row of ten girls on the left and seven boys on the right kneel in prayer, being all headless and therefore good children—if there be truth in the sign of "The Good Woman"—owing to the decapitating influences of the Cromwellian soldiery. They, of course, stabled their horses here, as they appear to have done in every church in England that has not been built since their time.

And yet no! I do remember one church in the fens of Lincolnshire, where the churchwarden had a primitive way of collecting for the Diffusion Society in his hat. There were some very fine old brasses there, and a genuine air of antiquity about the place. So I asked the clerk (who was, I'm afraid, not disposed in my favour, owing to my having infringed on his monopoly of the responses) whether he could tell me exactly where Cromwell's soldiers stabled their horses. "They hadn't been here," he assured me, innocently;

"at least *he* hadn't seen them! There was a young officer in the squire's pew a Sunday or two ago, but he didn't believe his name was anything like that, and he had walked from Alford, not ridden."

But I hold this to be the exception which proves the rule, that Cromwell's soldiers had nothing to do all the week but to look out a convenient church for their horses on the Sunday following.

Sir Jasper's tomb had, luckily, been spared by these omnipresent gentlemen. He reposed as comfortably as a gentleman can be supposed to do on the point of his left elbow, with a stiff ruff round his neck, a globe in one hand, and a sword in the other.

A marble canopy was raised over him, in front of which was represented, in bas-relief, the galleon—a most ungainly old tub, with an eruption of eight masts all over her, and two anchors hanging out at her stern.

Under the tablet recording his life and death, and those loveliest virtues and purest faiths which the Tresellans (if we may believe marble and brass) seem one and all to have possessed, was an allegorical bas-relief alluding to his absence at sea and his unexpected return; wherein a remarkably lively and uncrumpled Jonah was visible as far as his waist, in the jaws of what was intended for a whale, but was not very like a whale, for it was in shape like a camel, and backed like a weasel, and was, in fact, a griffin, without legs or wings. One thing, moreover, was clear: however big his head and ears, he never could have had sufficient abdominal accommodation for that very substantial Jonah. Indeed, the early artist had made so much prophet out of the first half of the figure, that it was quite a matter of conjecture as to how the legs could possibly be invested.

But though monuments are very fine things, and churches very proper places, and this one in particular is crowded with Tresellan records, I am afraid I must return to the living Tresellans, or I shall never get on with my story.

In the reign of George II., of blessed memory, who wore neat hessian boots, and ill-treated his wife in a manner which is, alas! not confined to kings, and was loved by her in return with an affection which is, I believe, almost peculiar to women, the head of the house of Tresellan was Sir Abel of that ilk.

He was a fine old gentleman of the true English sort; quick of temper, and slow of malice, with a hand as open as his face, and with as stout a muscle where his heart was, as anatomy ever had the fortune to meet with.

In his younger days he, with his brother-in-law, had got foolishly entangled in the Pretender's plots. The brother-in-law, Ernest Rewth, was killed in a skirmish, leaving two orphan children, of whom Abel became the second father, bringing them up with his two sons.

His first child, Aubyn, was the son of an Italian lady, whom Abel declared he had married in Italy. But, somehow, thanks to her dejected air and early death, as well as Sir Abel's apparent inability to bring any actual proof of its legality, the marriage grew to be questioned by his friends and neighbours, although no such whisper ever reached his ears, or those of his children, real or adopted. We all know how considerate people are, especially when, as in this case, the relater of the scandal would probably have been soundly kicked by the hearer.

Denzil, the second son, was born of an English mother, the widow of a near neighbour and old companion-in-arms. Sir Abel married her not long after the death of his first wife, as is the wont of middle-aged widowers of comfortable habits, who like to be "cared for."

Nothing could be more different than the dispositions of the two boys. Denzil, by some strange freak of nature, seemed to inherit Italian cunning and cruelty from Aubyn's mother—while her son was as English in face as he was in manner.

It only remains for me to describe the two adopted children. Frank Rewth was a handsome, harum-scarum lad, well fitted for the army, for which he was intended. I am sorry to say that a stay of some weeks with the officers of his future regiment sent him back, skilled in those arts of soldiercraft which were not taught by drill-sergeants, or written in books of military instruction. In a word, he could dice a little, and swear a little, and bet a little (though not about etymology), and drink a little. These were the vices of the army in the days of George II. remember. Now, *nous avons changé tout cela*; or, if we have not, I shall say nothing about it, having before my eyes the fear of the tall grenadier sentry afore-mentioned.

Emma Rewth was as pretty a little fairy as you ever set eyes on, and as wicked a witch as never footed on the Brocken Ranges. She had the loveliest of flaxen curls, dancing about her shoulders and catching every ray of sun in their neighbourhood. She had blue eyes and rosy cheeks—and a mouth. But the mouth, though finely chiselled, remarkably so for a fair woman, was a little too hard, and wanted that round softness for the loss of which its classic firmness did not atone.

The few years which she had spent under the care of Denzil's mother, did her character little good, I fear. That lady was rather weak, I take it, and apt to quarrel on slight grounds even with those she loved best. When she quarrelled with her husband, she was in the habit of flinging the cap off her head into the first convenient fire—it having been a part of the pin-money arrangement, that Sir Abel should keep her in head-gear.

The pin-money she used to lay by for "her Denzil," the younger son, of whom she used to speak as an injured being at times, when she suffered from an obsolete disease called "nerves," to cure which she took a something that was brought to her by fishermen's wives in black bottles, and was supposed not to have basked in the light of the eyes of his majesty's revenue officers, and of which Sir Abel knew nothing.

I feel this is very wicked tattle about the dear old soul; but then, you know, these extinct habits of our ancestors are invaluable to the body of antiquarians.

Every now and then, Denzil and the martyr of the nerves would have a little difference, and lo! within five hours after, a pedlar, or the keeper of some wretched little shop in Polvadnick, was sure to make his appearance at Tresellan, and Madam would lay out a heap of money (the hoard for the younger son) in such a miscellaneous collection of stores as would have ravished a magpie of the most versatile acquisitive habits. What an *omnium gatherum* of worthless rubbish was turned out, to be sure, when its purchaser departed for a world where is no pin-money and whither the Revenue does not extend its searches!

Emma, although a child, did not witness these outbursts of her aunt's temper without observing also their inefficacy, and the cause of it. Placing herself for the nonce in her aunt's position, she saw that the good lady stopped short just where her own spirit would have felt only a commencement.

One day, when the pedlar was there, under the usual circumstances, and Emma was urging her aunt to buy, the old lady was alarmed to find her niece's revenge outstripping hers, and she sent off the pedlar *instanter*.

"Buy, buy," said Emma, her eyes flashing and her lip trembling; "pour out the money—buy all!"

"Why, my dear Nem," said the aunt, "what do you mean? What are you thinking of, child?"

"If you mean to punish him," said Nem, sullenly tossing her head towards where she heard Denzil's voice in the hall, "why do you not spend every bit of it?" and she pointed to the drawer where the gold coins were lying.

"Because, my dear," said Lady Tresellan, whose weakness of character prevented her from seeing how injudicious it was to admit that the child had divined her purpose, just as it prevented her from being struck by the child's discovery; "because, my dear, I wish to frighten him—not to injure him, my poor Denzil!"

"I don't understand that. If I loved him I would not like to frighten him. And I do love him! But if I wished to punish him for quarrelling with me—look there!" and she jumped on a stool by the open window. "I would tie the money in a bag, and go to the end of the cliff yonder, and cast it right out into the sea!"

As she stood there, in the evening sunlight, she looked very beautiful—dangerously beautiful, like the green water under the window, rippling over the hidden peaks of the Sharphead Rocks.

"Come down, come down, child; you quite frighten me! What a little fury it is!" muttered the old lady.

I think she had a fit of the nerves immediately afterwards, but I know very well she never burnt her caps or bought rubbish in Emma's presence again after that. But it was too late! The seed was sown!

CHAPTER II.

THE SEA AND THE SEA-FOG.

WHEN Emma said she loved Denzil, she said no more than was true. From the moment when she and her brother were transferred to Tresellan she took a fancy to him.

But she openly owned to being the future wife of Aubyn. This she did of her own accord entirely, and further ratified the engagement by marking all her doll's clothes with A. T. The good-tempered, *laissez-faire* boy, made no protest, and seemed tolerably content to have his future planned with so little trouble to himself.

His father looked on it, first as a childish freak. But since, to his not very scrutinizing eye, the attachment seemed mutual and lasting, when the years rolled by the thing became talked of as settled, and Emma was looked on as the future Lady Tresellan.

That Aubyn did not love her, and, as he grew up, ceased even to be flattered by her election, I think was pretty evident from the little care he took to be with her. Nor was she, on the other hand, desirous of his company. As soon as Denzil's voice was heard returning (and when he grew to be a young man, his absences were long and frequent), Emma flew out to meet him and hear all his news (which, by the way, was little), and to pay him all those little attentions which are so delightful to man when received from a pretty girl, after an absence from home and home conveniences. Let him come when he would, he never failed to find a nicely-starched lace cravat, and a pair of fresh-whitened gloves ready for him in his bed-chamber.

Denzil was a handsome dandy, and you may be sure did not like these little attentions less because they came from another man's affianced, even though that man was his brother. To tell you the truth, he loved his brother no better than he did Emma, or, indeed, anybody else that we know of at present. But it suited his purpose to feign affection for "dear Nem," and he did so with an aptness that spoke him no novice in the art of deceiving women.

Poor Aubyn! what with his good-nature and his general trust in everybody, especially his brother and his cousins, he was completely blind to what another man would have seen in a moment—strangely blind.

So when Emma refused to kiss him night and morning, alleging that such familiarities were not allowed between engaged people, but saluted Denzil as a "dear brother," Aubyn only said, "Well, I think you might kiss me as well as Denzil, for I feel just like a brother to you, Nem."

At which ungallant speech Sir Abel laughed till he choked, and had to be revived with a tankard of morning ale.

Frank Rewth, the young reprobate, was, in the sense of being a fast little dog, more of a man of the world than our Aubyn. He made so free as to tell the latter that, "were he troth-plighted, he'd be hanged if any one lipped the girl but himself."

Aubyn answered, with his grave smile, "Dear old Frank, our Nem knows best. I could trust Denzil with my life; and had any but you, Frank, hinted this of your sister, why——" and he touched his sword, but with a merry smile.

Boys wore swords in those days, and those who wore swords did not often keep them long without getting them blood-rusty. Even Master Frank, lad though he was, had crossed rapiers with a tipsy cornet of dragoons for some foolish word-play with his name. So when Aubyn touched his hilt, Frank took off his hat, and drew his steel with a flourish, laughing all the while. So the two saluted, and then sheathed their blades again.

But when they parted at the ferry, over which Frank was going to tease the bare-legged fisher-girls on the other side, he said to Aubyn, with an air of much wisdom, "Have a care! Never trust a woman too much. I never met with one that was worth the price of a yard of ribbon, or was more to be trusted than a tuft of grass on the face of a cliff to save a man's life!"

Now, as Frank's experience of the fair sex went no further than a flirtation with the canteen-woman of the regiment he had visited, I think it desirable to chronicle an opinion so valuable.

Aubyn strolled back up the cliff again, and when he got to the top, he leant his arms on the rail that ran by the side, and looked out to sea.

The waters were very calm, and rolled in heavily like oil, scarcely breaking on the beach at all. The wind was little, and the sun feeble, and clouds of sea-fog were rolling toward the land. The Deadman's Head was lost to sight, while the promontory of Rame, far away on the other side, was becoming rapidly enshrouded too, for the mist was driving up the Channel. Some cold influences had condensed the humid vapours floating on the surface of the great Gulf Stream, as it swept by, fertilizing the far extremity of Cornwall, and had sent the rolling cloud in solemn march, from headland on to headland, before a south-westerly wind.

I do not know whether it was on account of the uninviting character of the view seaward; but before long Aubyn's eyes began to wander to a little cottage built on the quay, at the further end of the semicircle, in which the town nestled.

This was the residence of Christopher Pentowan, the lawyer. His office was at the side of the house, opposite the Ship Inn, the sign of which, by the by, appeared to be a careful copy of the great galleon on Sir Jasper's tomb.

Christopher Pentowan was a lawyer after the devil's own heart—a money-lender, a devourer of the poor, an oppressor. Town scandal added to these titles the further one of smuggler. For in those days smuggling was a profession much followed; and many a suspicious vessel hovered about the mouth of Polvadnick harbour, in spite of the watch and ward held by Sir Abel Tresellan, J.P., and conservator of the customs of his gracious Majesty George II.

You have probably pictured this usurer as a lean Shylock; but you are wrong. He was a fat-faced, rosy, double-chinned fellow, with a deep, full voice. His sentences rolled out round, sleek, oily, and seeming-savoury, as you may note sausages issue from a patent machine. Great was this hero at public meetings and festive dinners, but greatest at small festivities. Happy was he who sat in company with him, and reposed beneath his calm glory. To look at him, you could not have believed it possible that this man was really a Shylock. And yet he was. True, he never did actually cut his own dinner out of his clients' persons; but he served their hearts so cruelly that I don't think he would have cared much about any number of pounds of the flesh nearest to it.

His face, fat as it was, and crowned with black ringlets, had an air of handsome vulgarity; and, if he had lived to our time, he was the sort of man to wear an expansive white waistcoat and a double shirt-frill, and to make excruciating puns at small tea-parties in a Sir Oracle voice.

"And can this man be a rogue?" you ask me. I am sorry to say, yes. And yet he had his good point, for if he devoured widows' houses, he cer tainly never made long prayers, whether as a pretence or otherwise.

In one thing he resembled "Jephthah, judge of

Israel." For "he had one fair daughter, and no more, the which he loved passing well!" And she, by that merciful arrangement of woman's nature, for which we men can never be sufficiently grateful, did not see his faults and sins; but clung to the old reprobate as fondly as if he had been the best creature in the world.

Lucinda Pentowan was a handsome girl—not one of your flaxen-haired dolls, but a tall, straight woman, with black hair and dark eyes. Her arm was an arm of flesh and blood, the latter running pretty visibly under the brown skin. As for her hand, she could not have squeezed it into the largest "six and a half" gloves that ever were made—for she was no *mignonne*. There was something queenly about this lady; and in looking at her picture, I feel, as I do when I see that of Mrs. Siddons—"This was a woman to live and die for, who would live and die for the man she chose."

It was to catch a glimpse of this figure, possibly, that Aubyn turned his eyes towards the cottage, and he certainly watched it for a long time; until, with a start, he recovered from his reverie, and shaking his head, turned down the path to the ferry.

He had been so buried in thought that he had

not observed Sir Abel's passing him as he stood there.

Sir Abel, as I have told you, had been in Italy. As a youth, he had been somewhat of a wanderer; and the see-saw of life had gone up and down with him pretty often.

I don't think he was a sad man, or wished to have his past life back again. Men of his age do not do that, I fancy.

I remember, at the university, when I was crossed in love, or crossed at the kitchen and buttery, and had to send out for my dinner to the incomparable Bickerstaff, that I had a way of smoking a gloomy pipe, and quoting, from some quarter or other, the line—

> "Hei mihi preteritos referret si Jupiter annos."

Now, if I am sick and sorry, I don't always take the pipe, and I *never* take the quotation. Why should Jupiter refer our preterite years to us? I'm afraid we should not do much good with the remittance.

And so, though Sir Abel was a grave man, I don't think he was a sad one; for he was content that the past should be past, and he had a modest hope and belief in his future.

There were times, though, when he was fain to

get away from the presence of his second wife, and to carry his thoughts out to sea.

Then he would go down to the beach, and taking the porter's lad with him, put out his little sailing-boat, and skim away before the wind. He continued this habit after his wife's death.

When he passed Aubyn, he was going on this very errand, and was, I believe, as unconscious of his son's presence as his son was of his.

The mist was still flying along the channel. Now and then a skirl of wind would lift it for a moment, and then down it settled again.

One such momentary clearance showed Sir Abel's well-known boat to the knot of fishers gathered at "the town-head," as the space between the church and the sea-wall was called.

"Eh, lads!" said one gray-headed old man, "I'd a gi'en my next catch o' mackerel not to ha' seed yon boat out to-day!"

"How so, Cap'n Jack?" was the general inquiry.

The old man was looked on with great awe by the superstitious fishermen, for he was held to have second-sight.

"Well, then, ye do know as how as Sir Jasper were wrecked on to Sharpyhead yonder——"

"Ay, sure; and he were mad, and 'tis in the family now, I reck'n," added several; while one murmured—"Ess, and some o' 'em ha' gone mazed since, and they all begin wi' the same words, some'at about 'say-dogs,' so I've a heerd 'em say."

"Well, then!" said the old fisherman, who had waited patiently for perfect silence, "this very morn, as I comed down to carr' my nets to barkin', I seed a great ship (so large as the church 'twere), and it comed in right on to Sharpy-head, and then I seed some one come right out to bowspurt-end, and throw up his arms. And then it all sinked away into the mist. I tell 'ee I seed un so plain as I see yon hosgead o' pilchers!" and he pointed to a neighbouring barrel of those delicacies.

The little group loitered about in the hope of hearing more, but the aged prophet was silent. He continued to mend his net, an occupation which he had interrupted when the sudden shifting of the sea-fog revealed Sir Abel's boat.

Half an hour after, as the old man got up from his seat by the pilot's hut, the report of a gun, deadened to a dull flap, like the sound of a bird's wing, reached his ear. The sound was very dead, and hardly waked an echo in the many-hollowed valley of the Perl.

"Ay, ay, Mas'r Denzil," said the gray-haired fisherman, "there ye are firin' on they poor choughs, that ne'er harmed you nor yourn. God send that they poor birds' homes may be the on'y ones where there'll be wailin' to-day!"

Now, as Master Denzil did not happen to be out shooting choughs, as any one might have concluded after a moment's consideration of the thickness of the fog, I will leave my readers to believe or not, as they choose, in that second-sight of the old man's, for which all his neighbours gave him credit.

Meanwhile, Sir Abel and the boy were skimming away out to sea, the boat, "with a bone in her teeth," now running up the long side of the swell, and then, after a pause amid the foam at the crest, hissing down on the other side. There was no boat along the coast that could touch the "Dark Lady" when she heeled over before the wind, and dashed along with a wall of water, two handsbreadths high, above her leeward quarter.

The "Dark Lady" was running on the starboard tack, when Sir Abel, with a sudden grasp of the tiller, brought her round trembling and quivering before the wind. The cause of this sudden manœuvre lay before him. A long, low, rakish-looking vessel was lying-to about a quarter of a mile from him; while, between him and it, a boat, piled with bales, and rowed slowly by eight oarsmen, was making toward the shore.

In a moment Sir Abel read the meaning of all this. The smugglers had taken advantage of the fog to bring their vessel as close in-shore as they dared, and were now unloading her cargo, which seemed a large and valuable one.

With Sir Abel there was no question as to what he should do. He was alone, and unarmed, it was true, but he was a justice of the peace, and he could never allow the rascals to land their run right under his very nose.

Besides, the story would be told about him, for such stories *did* creep into good society in those days. So he bore right down on to the boat; and standing up when he got within hailing distance, he summoned the crew to surrender in the king's name.

A loud laugh was the only answer he got. But as he still kept overhauling them, one of the crew stood up and shouted out, "We know you, Sir Abel; but keep off, or, by heaven, we'll fire into you!"

"Fire away, and be cursed!" said Sir Abel, his noble old face lighting up. "It shall never be said I let a scum of rats land under my very nose!"

"Keep off, Sir Abel!" cried another voice; "there are those here that can't let you see them and live. If you value your life, put about!"

"Cowardly dogs! let them face me like men, and I'll meet them, and punish them with my own hand, on sea or land, and keep their secret till then!"

You must remember at the time when this challenge was given, the gentry knew a great deal about running cargoes, and were not loath to lend their cellars for purposes of concealment; nay, pulled an oar themselves at times of a dark night perhaps.

The only answer to Sir Abel's defiance was another warning. And then as his boat came nearer, a rosy round face, with a hat pressed down over its forehead, appeared over the heap of bales in the middle of the boat.

The warning was repeated, but was again unheeded, for Sir Abel was trying to identify the fresh face.

"Your blood on your own head, Abel Tresellan!" said a deep, rich voice, and Sir Abel saw the glint of a gun-barrel.

He never flinched. As he stood up there in the bows, with the water hissing at his feet, he only smiled gravely. And the whole of his past life, and the light of the faith of a true Christian and English gentleman, flashed before his eyes in a second.

"Lord have mercy! I am doing my duty!" he whispered. And then the shot rang out! Sir Abel fell back on the thwarts, a martyr to those miserable laws, that, like the game-laws of our time, were rather temptations than prohibitions: laws that made the lives of "men with mothers dear," and "men with sisters and wives," the price of the lace that fluttered on my lady's shoulders, or the silk that whispered about her dainty feet.

When Sir Abel sank back in the boat, the poor frightened lad with him put about with all speed, as he was bid to do by those in the larger boat.

Kneeling in the bottom of the skiff, he took his kind master's head in his lap, and wiped the foam from his lips, and strove to staunch the blood that came oozing out of the bullet-wound in his side.

Presently the Head at Tresellan looked down upon them from out of the fog; and soon the little boat, with a trembling sail, as if conscious of its terrible burden—a dying man—lay-to alongside of Polvadnick pier.

Loud was the lament among the fishers of Polvadnick when they saw the plight of their patron. As soon as they gathered the already half-guessed truth from the boy, the pilot-boat was manned, and the coast to westward searched, but no sign was seen either of schooner or boat.

Meanwhile, with careful tread, four stout men carried their wounded master home on a rude litter made of oars and old sails.

Tho gray-headed seer was among the busiest in the construction of this, and spent all his care in so arranging the canvas that no blood should fall on the stones, muttering to himself an old local rhyme—

"The clear shall seem dark, and the dark shall seem clear,
When the blood of Tresellan is red on the pier."

And as Sir Abel was lifted from the skiff, a single drop fell among the slippery weed, and ran away out of sight unnoticed.

CHAPTER III.

OF MARRIAGE AND OLD MORSE.

When the breakfast party broke up at Tresellan, on the morning when my story begins, Denzil slipped away, purposely evading the eyes of Emma. He got into a boat and pulled up the Perl until he came to an old summer-house, called the "Lady's Tryst," which commanded a noble view of the junction of the Glese with the Perl. Here he landed, and struck across country, skirting the oak-woods. At length he turned back again towards the river, and, descending by a narrow bridle-path, came to a cottage, which, though close by the water-side, was as completely concealed from the view of any one on the Perl, as if it had been surrounded by a wall of mountain.

Now, I quite agree with the reader that it looks very suspicious to see a young man dodging about like this, and at last running to earth in a secret hut.

So we shall not be surprised, on entering the

room, close at his heels, to see my gentleman submitting to the caresses of a good-looking woman, who has a gold ring on the third finger of her left hand, and who calls him "Bud!"

Yes, Denzil was secretly married!

His wife was a tall, spare, but still (as I described her) good-looking woman. I should say there must have been ten years' difference in their ages—and the difference was on the wrong side.

Martha Tresellan had deep lines about her eyes that told of old troubles, and there was a nervous action about her mouth which did not wear a very sweet smile, though a smile it did wear. It seemed as though her lips scorned themselves for the hypocrisy of it.

Cannot you easily see when a woman loves a man? Her looks, though they do not, perhaps, dwell long, yet say and read much. She almost imperceptibly leans on him, and seems dependent, knowing that by so doing she makes him proud—and pride is half a man's love.

There was none of this to be seen in Martha. Self-included, self-reliant, she stood, and allowed herself to be loved, rather than met affection half-way.

The history of lives is often revealed in minute actions. I seem to read in this woman's independent position towards her husband a very sad tale. A tale of a heart once too reposing, too confiding —but a heart bruised and cicatrized by that first deceiving, so as never to feel the like again. Denzil—sharp, shrewd, Denzil—did not he see this? Not a bit of it; he conceived his wife to be a model of love and trust, and all that is matrimonially desirable.

I should not wonder if some critical reader should draw a parallel between Denzil's blindness and that of Aubyn's, mentioned before. I confess the repetition to be there, but I do not think it could truthfully be otherwise. Who sees most of the game? Who sees least of the deception that is being practised? Don't all our friends always see much clearer into our affairs than we do? (For if they don't, why should they always be troubling themselves about them?) And then, moreover, Denzil was in love, and love is proverbially blind; and Aubyn was just as foolish as if he had been in love, being, according to the old song, one of those "who trust too much."

Where Denzil met with his wife, I am not quite able to discover, for the Tresellan records in which I have traced out this story, were much damaged, seven years ago, by the fire that destroyed the left wing of the building.

I imagine they must have made each other's acquaintance at the shire-town at some fair or public festivity.

From the few old brown ragged letters, breathing long-dead love, to which I refer for this part of my tale, I gather the old, old story—though rather a new version of it. The betrayer became the betrayed, for Denzil was young, and Martha was experienced in the ways of the world. He wooed, and she feigned to love; and then, when she discovered "how cruelly he would have deceived her," the only way he saw to repair his mistake was to marry her—as the prudent Martha had all along imagined and intended.

So at the age of eighteen Denzil was a Benedict, and he managed to keep his wife at the little cottage on the Perl, and what was more, to conceal her from every eye for two years. Here, then, was the reason of Denzil's frequent and long absences from home—here was the secret of his indifference to Emma's love. And, what is more, here was the hidden trouble that made his brow dark, and went far to aggravate the bad points in his character.

But as long as he stayed at the concealed cottage, he was perfectly happy. His indolent, selfish nature was not disturbed by his self-dependent wife, who was not in love with him enough to let her desires clash with his. Having no real affection, though with quite enough of its semblance to deceive this inexperienced boy, Martha was never carried away by her feelings. In a word, she passed her married life not as a loving woman does, but rather as a crafty mechanic regulates a delicate piece of machinery, oiling a wheel here, easing a band there, and so avoiding the destruction which any disarrangement would bring with it.

Only once did Denzil and his wife have words. It was when he came down one day, and found a brown-eyed, rough-headed boy gambolling on the little lawn, and his wife watching him from the window. It was the nearest risk of discovery he ever ran, for the lad was one of those always scrambling half-naked among the pools and rocks of the Polvadnick shore.

"What do you want with that devil's imp, Matty, unless you wish to put an end to our secret?" he asked, rather fiercely, when he reached the room, having entered the house from the back.

"Devil's imp yourself!" said Martha, an unexplainable fury flashing in her eyes. "It's little pleasure I see here, and why may I not have the child to amuse me? He's more amusing and better-looking than you are!"

Denzil burst out into a laugh, for he fancied his wife must be joking. But she was not, though Denzil's laugh gave her time to feign that she was.

So, with a graver face, she said, "Well, jesting apart, the child came down and found the place out, and I have given him some cake, and promised him more if he will never bring anybody here, and self-interest will keep him quiet."

So the first storm of Denzil's married life passed over, and left no trace. But had I been in his place, unless I had been very much in love, I should have been struck by Martha's sudden rage, and her remark about the boy. I am sure I should not have liked the clutch she made at her bosom, as if she carried a knife there.

From that time Denzil became accustomed to see the urchin at times about the place, and he forgot all about the little tiff.

He might have seen, when the lad was there, how his wife watched him, and it might have set him wondering, but he was too indolent and too well satisfied with his wife's attention to care to keep his eyes very wide open. He mistook this attention for affection, as I have said before, and

I believe he found it far more pleasant than he would have found the real feeling, which has its requirements as well as its concessions.

But I have been relating the commencement of Denzil's married life, instead of confining myself to the particular morning on which we have followed him up the Perl to Lady's Tryst, and on to the secluded cottage.

After the first kiss, Denzil threw himself on a lounge by the window, and Martha, sitting on a low stool by his side, filled him a pipe of tobacco, and lit it. For this young man had learnt, in heaven only knows what disreputable haunts, to indulge in the Indian weed, though he never did so at Tresellan. This gave an additional zest to his wedded happiness. (I think if ladies generally would believe this statement, they might take a large per centage of cases off the overburdened hands of Sir C. C.)

While her lord and master solaced himself with the fragrance of his Virginia, Martha betook herself again to her sewing, watching him from the corners of her eyes. This said "sewing" was the cutting and contriving of fine cambric, flannel, and lace, into little white garments, somewhat too large for a doll of ordinary proportions.

They would have been a pleasant picture, this couple, if they had not seemed each so absorbed in self, and had there not been that disparity of age and experience that was plainly visible in their faces.

"Where is your ragged *protégé*, Matty?" said the husband. "I think he would look well in this little cap!" and he held the jimcrack up on the point of his finger. He was looking at that so that he could not see the expression of pain flit across his wife's face, and dim her eyes for a moment.

"Oh! he has not been here to-day—he tells me when the fog is at sea, he is on the water too. I suppose he amuses himself with fraudulent forays on the lobster-pots or the stake-nets."

Denzil laughed, but his laugh stopped very suddenly!

It seemed at first as if it were only the noise of the woods, but it grew more plain presently, and then the sound of a bell came quivering into the still air of that cool room shaded with overhanging boughs, and heavy with the perfume of the limes.

Well did Denzil know that sound, and he sprang to his feet, and then stood motionless as a statue.

That bell was swaying to and fro in the centre turret of Tresellan.

That bell had rung when the news came that the Tresellan was lying cold, with his face to the stars, on the field of Hastings.

That bell had rung when the crusader closed his weary eyes in the home of his fathers.

That bell had rung when Sir Philip's funeral cavalcade wound up to the hall from the ferry. It had rung while Sir Jasper's body was stretched yet undiscovered, in the gray morning, on the shingle of the Polvadnick beach. It had rung when Sir Geoffrey, the cup-bearer, was lying dead in his master's palace.

In a word, it was a bell that, from time unremembered, had tolled for the head of the Tresellans.

The crones in the neighbourhood declared that the strongest tempest could not shake the crazy old turret where it hung, but that even in the quietest night of summer, if death was about to claim "the Tresellan," a single, low breath of wind came across the sea, woke the voice of the bell once, and no more, and passed away over the hills into the bosom of the darkness.

But you must not think from this that Sir Abel was dead. When he was carried to his room, and the old doctor pronounced that he was in a very dangerous state, Emma was present. She was the mistress of the house, in the fact of being the only woman there when sorrow came, so she led the leech up to the wounded man's room, and awaited his decision.

As soon as she heard it, she left the chamber and sped along the gallery to the turret-stair. Just as she opened the door, the old butler, the tears running down his furrowed cheeks, caught hold of her skirt, crying, "Is he dead, then?" "No, not dead, but like to die," was the hurried answer, for Emma wanted to get rid of every impediment in the way of her ringing the bell.

"Sure, Miss Emma, you are never going to toll Old Morse while the master has a hope of life?" Old Morse (probably a corruption of Mors) was the name the bell went by among the people about Tresellan.

But in vain were the butler's entreaties and warnings, though seconded by those of the housekeeper, for Emma had set her heart on ringing the bell, as she fancied it would recall Denzil, and this Rebekah was determined that her favourite should come and seek a blessing before his father died.

So up she sped round the winding stair,

frightening the noisy jackdaws off their nests, as she crashed over the cracking sticks collected on the steps. And now she reached the belfry under the great bell, and as she swayed and swayed at the rope, she saw it begin to tremble and move, and at last, after two faint strokes, the clang burst out full and clear, making the turret tremble at its note, and the rope quiver in her hands.

I think if she had known where the sound of that bell would find Denzil, she would have twisted that cord very tightly round her own neck before she would have consented to pull it.

CHAPTER IV.

LAST REQUESTS.

WITH scarce an explanation to his wife, Denzil plunged down the stairs, and rushed towards home. This time he ran straight along the river-bank. As he neared the Lady's Tryst, he heard Aubyn calling him by name, and in a moment more they stood face to face.

"So you have dogged my footsteps!" was the first burst of Denzil's uncontrollable anger, and he lost all recollection of the bell. But his brother's voice recalled him. Laying his hand on his arm, Aubyn said, "Don't say that, Denzil; you will be very sorry directly. I never dogged your footsteps, but when I was out in the woods shooting one day, I saw you pass this way, and I have always seen you coming and going this way. I have not tried to learn why. If you conceal it, it is doubtless for a good reason, and I respect it. But, Denzil, our father has been shot by smugglers, and he is dying, and when I heard that Emma had begun to ring the bell (I could wish we might have let you know somehow else), I set off in this direction to meet you."

"Is he dead?"

"No. Did not I tell you so?—it was careless of me. But, I fear, mortally wounded."

While this conversation was passing, they had gained the bank, and were soon seated in the boat. Once there, all talking ceased, for both put their strength forth to make it fly over the water, down to Tresellan.

They were received with silence, for the servants, one and all, were cowed and uncomfortable at the thought of Emma's ringing the bell. Indeed, they seemed to shun her, as if she had been the cause of Sir Abel's calamity. Even Sir Abel himself felt a sudden shock when the sound smote his ear.

"What did you ring it for, Nem?" he asked, with a voice that had an accent of sorrow and surprise in it. "I heard it when my poor father died, and I thought I should never hear it again. But never mind—cheer up, child. An hour or so sooner or later, what consequence?"

When Aubyn and Denzil arrived, the former assumed enough of the headship of the house to get rid of the Reverend James Sterrup, the parson of Polvadnick. For this worthy divine, when he came to do his office by Sir Abel's bedside, had his wig awry, and was husky in the voice, as how should he not be? For had he not been sitting in the "Ship" parlour, with the Romanist captain of the Mediterranean vessel then in harbour? and was not his theological controversy carried on, in every sense, with great spirit?

A far better historian than I has told you of the little foibles of these good men. Happy are we that there are no such foibles among them now; and that if the lads at college be vinous, and fond of good cheer, they put these childish things by anon, and address themselves earnestly and humbly to the noblest duty on the face of the earth.

Sterrup was a good specimen of his class, for, if he did discuss much besides theology at the "Ship," you saw nothing of it in the church on Sunday, when he preached excellent sermons. That he could scarcely help doing, for like the sun revolving through the signs of the zodiac, he travelled each year through those sermons of the well-known old divines that are still the models followed by our clergy. (Indeed, some of them even go so far as to photograph these models.)

Not without a little difficulty—for Sterrup had a great idea of doing his duty—Aubyn managed to get rid of him, and then returned to his father.

Sir Abel, propped up with pillows, took the hand of each of his sons in his, while Emma leant on the bed with her arm round Frank, who seemed in an utter bewilderment, and was as helpless as a child.

With his family thus grouped round him, Sir Abel began in a faint voice a narrative, of which, as I fear I cannot give it you in his words, I purpose to show you a condensed sketch.

In his earlier days, while travelling in Italy on the Pretender's errands, Sir Abel had met with a lovely girl in one of the convents, into which his mission took him.

A mutual affection was the fruit of a very few interviews, and he learnt with regret that Isabel was heir to a large fortune, to ensure which for the church the crafty priesthood had obtained from her dying father a command that his child should take the veil.

It was long before Sir Abel could contrive to overcome her unwillingness to disobey her parent's dying words, and, when that obstacle was removed, another presented itself. Who would marry them? He searched high and low among the priests for one who would perform the ceremony. He offered bribes of large amount to some of those known not to be over scrupulous. But even these itching fingers dreaded to meddle with what was looked on as church property. The result of Sir Abel's attempts was that the lady was confined to her cell, and he got a pretty broad hint to leave the convent.

He did so at once, like a sensible man, for resistance would only have increased his difficulties. But he did not leave the neighbourhood. In various disguises, learnt in the Pretender's service, he hung about the convent, and hoped to be able, at some future period, to carry Isabel to England, where he would have found no obstacle to their marriage.

But just when all seemed most hopeless, appeared a *deus ex machinâ* in the person of an uncle of Isabel's. He was a poor priest of the order of St. Francis, who had devoted himself to the church on the death of his betrothed. Some lingering sparks of love and sympathy were still latent in his breast; indeed, he was not an old man, and the sight of these unhappy lovers set his yet warm blood tingling with sympathy. In confession, he learned from Isabel her intention of flying with her lover to England, and fearful lest her confidence in Sir Abel might be misplaced, he determined, like old Friar Laurence, in "Romeo and Juliet," to wed the young couple. As a proof of Abel's singleness of purpose, he asked of him a promise not to seek for his wife's riches, but to allow them to flow in their intended channel.

The marriage was performed secretly. Before the altar they all vowed never to reveal when, where, and by whom it was performed, save under certain conditions.

In these days we can scarcely understand the necessity of this precaution. But at that period, the powerful "Society of Jesus" spread its arms far and wide through every land, Romanist or Protestant. Short would have been the shrift of our Franciscan had his part in the matter been suspected. It is almost incredible to believe the constant apprehension Sir Abel lived under, that every foreign vessel which touched at Polvadnick brought some agent of the mystic brotherhood, commissioned to perform goodness knows what vengeance on the contemners of the Church's power and wisdom.

No wonder the poor lady paled and grew thinner daily with this terrible curse hanging over her. When a strange ship came into the harbour, she retired to her own chamber, and was not seen out of doors again until some days after the suspected craft had sailed.

This was the story which, with much difficulty and with many pauses, for the tears were rolling down his cheeks, Sir Abel disclosed to his children. When he had concluded it, he added, "And now, Aubyn, your title to Tresellan must be confirmed. I do not wish a stranger to do the office, but either you, or Denzil, or Frank, must journey to Italy, find out Brother Seraphicus, and giving him my ring, tell him that I, the widower, on my deathbed, asked him for the proof of my son's legitimacy."

"It shall be done, sir," said Aubyn; "but let me place you back on the bed; the long time you have been speaking has wearied you; you look pale." But his father declined the offer, and raising himself on his left hand, looked round into the faces about his bed. His voice was hollow and faint when he spoke again.

"Frank and Emma, dear children, Tresellan will always be your home; *yours*, indeed, Emma;" and he laid her hand in Aubyn's; but it did not close on hers, which lay cold and passionless in it.

"Aubyn, my brave son, remember your name! Let Tresellan be the refuge of the oppressed, and its master the friend of all, rich or poor. For you, Denzil, I have but the younger brother's portion of an empty blessing to give you; but I have such faith in my Aubyn that I do not fear for you."

"He shall be no less lord of Tresellan than I, father," murmured Aubyn.

"But, beware," continued the dying man, "beware, Denzil, of the dark spirit that even my old eyes have seen in you. Be open as the day, love your brother, forsake not a friend; hate evil passions as you would hate your worst enemy—but *him* forgive. Ah! Denzil, Denzil, I have more fear for your disposition than for any of the others. Attend to and think of my last words: and if ever you listen to sin, and wrong those that love you, the curse——"

Here the poor gentleman, who had become far too much excited during the last part of his farewell to his children, fell back on his pillow. A violent cough followed, and his mouth became filled with blood. They raised him in haste, but the spirit was fled. Noble in deed and word, with scarce an enemy in the world, with friends unnumbered to lament him, this honest, Christian gentleman passed away. So they laid this true son of England to sleep in his native land, in the church where they had borne him to be enrolled in the Christian army—among his ancestors, whose great deeds of arms and feats of valour read but coldly when compared with the true record of his honest life.

The four orphans stood for a while beside the death-bed—then one by one stole out.

Aubyn betook him to his own room, and gave way to a passionate burst of tears, until sleep brought him a transient calm. When a man sheds tears, remember, it is a very different thing from that ready overflow that gives relief to a woman's sorrow. Every drop scalds his eyes, and is the birth of infinite throes and agonies, until the physical exhaustion renders sleep absolutely necessary; and oh, how calming and refreshing is that sleep after tears!

Denzil passed from the room closely followed by Emma. As she turned to go to her chamber, she laid her hand on his shoulder, and looking into his face with tearless eyes, whispered, "The curse was not spoken, Denzil dear!" And so she disappeared, and sitting alone revolved such thoughts in that dark heart of hers, as must have made even herself shudder had they been revealed to her in the full light of day. But she was only half-conscious of her own meditations—a half-awakened Eve with the toad squatted by her ear.

Denzil went out into the yard. He, too, was wrapt in thought. The result of such pre-occupation of mind is often very strange; but surely Denzil's heart could not have been deeply stirred, or he would never have been guilty of the conduct of which I am going to tell you.

As he stepped into the yard, one of the stable-helpers was seated by the door on a saddle-tree. He touched his cap with sorrowful respect. Denzil turned to him with, "Charles, the gray horse has a loose shoe. See that it is looked to!"

The lad touched his cap again; but he shrugged his shoulders when Denzil's back was turned, and said to himself, "Well! be sure, you're making out who's master quick, and poor Sir Abel scarce cold yet!"

As for poor Frank Rewth, he was, without exception, the most miserable creature in the whole house. With red eyes and blubbered cheeks he wandered up stairs and down, seeking comfort from all he could meet.

He finished by sitting by the fire in the old housekeeper's room, where he drowned his feelings in such a copious supply of mulled wine, that I am afraid, poor fellow! he was not a very reputable object when he went to bed.

How could he help it? His weak, fond nature turned for comfort to the other sex, as might have been expected, and the housekeeper and all the women-servants pitied him, and pressed mulled consolation upon him, and believed in their hearts he was the only one of the four children who regretted Sir Abel.

Demonstrative grief is very often credited for far too great depth, and still, deep waters of sorrow are allowed to flow on unnoticed by a foolish world, that judges by profession rather than acts, and is satisfied with the inspection of the outside of things, without caring to pierce any deeper.

Aubyn was sorry to find his cousin in this state, but excess in wine was so prevalent then it was scarce thought a vice.

So Aubyn saw poor Frank safely to bed, and left him to finish by himself in the darkness the long harangue he had been making.

"He loved Aubyn next best to poor Sir Abel—he did, by heaven!—and he'd prove it. He would prove it on anybody. He was no coward, if his eyes were red. Coward! would he not pour out his best blood for Aubyn? Would he not stand and fall by him in right or wrong, good or evil? And, by heaven! if he would set him a task to try his true affection, he would do it, or die in the attempt."

This, and much more to the same purpose, he poured into Aubyn's ears, as long as he was in the room, and after his departure, bestowed on his own coat, hanging on a chair, which he imagined to be his cousin, and upon which he lavished endless vows of friendship and protestations of fidelity.

And at last sleep came to all in Tresellan, and the whole great house was hushed and silent —as hushed and silent as the calm white face of Sir Abel lying on the pillows of the great bed in the state chamber.

CHAPTER V.

LADY MACBETH.

Early next morning Denzil was seated in the south window of the great hall, looking seaward at the lazy gulls dipping their wings in the rippled water. A gentle air came shaking the short dry grass on the cliff, and swept in at the window, blowing cool upon his forehead.

A light hand was on his shoulder, and he knew that Emma was beside him. What was the community of thought between these two, that made them look so guiltily in each other's faces?

Their meditations had been on the same subject all night. Sorrow had not sent them to sleep with wet eyelids. Care and avarice and passion had stretched them on the rack from one weary chiming of the clock to another, until the stars grew pale, and the noise of the twittering birds began the *reveillé* of life.

No wonder, then, that Denzil flung open his vest as he sat in the fresh breeze,—no wonder that the roses in Emma's cheeks did not unfold until the wind had saluted them tolerably roughly.

These two, being conscious each that the other's predominant feeling was not grief, but something between curiosity and anxiety about Sir Abel's first marriage, did not feign sorrow when they met.

"Have you thought it over, Denzil?" were Emma's first words.

"I've been doing nothing else ever since," he answered, "and I cannot understand—or misunderstand—or leave off trying to read the riddle!"

"I see no riddle in it," was the reply. "I see your way to wealth and power;"—and then she stopped.

Denzil rose, and walked up and down the hall several times, watching Emma out of the corners of his downcast eyes, and waiting for her to continue. And this tiny woman, looking, I protest to you, like a fairy, with the faintest rose in her cheeks, and her curls blown about by the amorous wind, stood there quite still, wearing ever so slight a smile on her lips.

That smile was the smile of triumph at an ascertained fact.

When you, disciple of "Gentle Izaak" (who sewed live frogs on cruel hooks), wandering in the country, come upon a nameless stream, overhung with willows, and wrinkled here and there with an eddy, what do you do? You take out your finest tackle, and adjust the limber-rod. Next, the fly goes spinning along the water—again and again. Presently, there is a dimple in a quiet nook of the stream, and an acute-angled ripple makes its way toward the fly.

Then a smile comes twitching at the corner of your mouth, and twinkles in your eyes, for you know you have not cast your fly upon waters that are untenanted.

I have no doubt that, when a certain nameless personage goes a-fishing for souls, he smiles when his poor prey begin to nibble; and I fancy his smile would be not unlike that which Emma gave as she watched Denzil.

Denzil's meditations, all the night through, had been rather retrospective than prospective. As he tossed and fretted on his sleepless bed, he had only said, "Alas! for the past."

He wished that his father had never visited Italy, and, becoming morbidly righteous and loyal, as men do when they have committed or are about to commit sin and dishonour, he began to look on the misery of Sir Abel's marriage as a punishment arising wholly from his connection with the Pretender. The utmost that Denzil dared to think, speculatively, went no further than a hope that Father Seraphicus might be dead, or otherwise lost to mortal ken.

It was not thus with Emma.

The first question which her mind proposed to itself was, "What can be done?"

The past was past, the dead were dead, but she and her passion and her ambition were yet alive.

At first, this was hardly revealed to herself as a planning of evil, but, as the night wore away, and the darkness rolled back from the earth, another darkness gathered about her heart, and, at last, she was not ashamed to acknowledge to herself the wrong she was meditating.

The only plea she put forward to her own soul was a poor one. As the magnitude of the crime she was pondering broke upon her, she sat up in the bed, and, with something like tears gathering in her eyes, cried out, "I was nursed in luxury, the pet and the spoilt child, and I love him, I love him; oh! how dearly! I cannot consent to wed the younger son—no! not if I break off the contract with his brother. Of course we should be turned out of Tresellan. And yet, oh! Denzil, Denzil—I will be yours—I *must* be yours!"

After this passionate outbreak, for passionate it was, not in spite of, but in the fact of, its being composed of such homely words, she fell back on the pillow, and as daylight looked in at the window, snatched a short and troubled sleep.

About the same time, Denzil too stole a brief slumber, as it were, out of the very bosom of the morning. By a strange magnetic sympathy his last thought was, "I will see what Emma says to-day."

So when they met, this Lady Macbeth, this dagger wreathed with rose leaves, watched at the first cast to see if her bait was likely to be taken. Women's eyes are sharp, and wickedness does not blind them; so she knew at a glance that Denzil was ready to take and eat of the fruit which her hand had gathered.

After a time, finding she did not speak again, Denzil stopped his walk, and, turning to her, asked, with a hoarse voice, "My way to wealth and power! How?"

"By making stepping-stones of fools," said the bitter little lady; and the smile still played about her lips.

"I'm not clever, Nem; tell me what you mean."

"I mean that I would have wit inherit the place of folly. Will Aubyn do honour to the name of Tresellan? He will idle away his life watching the fishing-boats, and spend his patrimony in clothing fishers' brats, whose nature it is to go naked. But you, Denzil, should rule here. There is more sense in your boot than in his whole body. You look the gentleman, and are the gentleman. He looks the boor, and his looks do not belie him!"

"This of your future husband, Nem!" interrupted Denzil, for his vanity could not resist the remark even at such a moment. But he repented saying it, for Emma turned on him such a look of fire as no one could believe blue eyes capable of. But she did not notice his interruption in words.

"I have been thinking over Sir Abel's orders, and it seems to me that Frank is the most trustworthy person to go in search of Father Seraphicus." And the smile was still on her lips, but the expression was varied a little. "Frank is steady and quiet, and is so careful that he is not likely to lose what is entrusted to his care. And even were he not so, I cannot see how either you or Aubyn (the parties interested) could go, without giving ground for wrong interpretations."

"But will Aubyn consent to this?"

"Will he not listen to my lightest command? He is well-trained in that, at least, to do him credit. And when my words condescend to become arguments, I think he will not only obey, but be convinced."

"By Jove! you look like a queen, Nem!"

The smile changed again. It was very sweet, even in the midst of that compact of evil, in that hurried arrangement of plans, to hear this candid praise from such beloved lips.

The feelings thus awakened made her tender, and for a moment she pitied even Aubyn. She sighed softly, "Poor fellow! how wretched he will be to lose me, and to find I never loved him!"

But she was mistaken there. Let us hope the pity, like blessings and curses, returned to her again; for she needs it—and will need it sorely.

Denzil either did not hear or did not choose to hear this; but there was a tone of irritation in his voice when he spoke again.

"But I don't see my 'way to power and wealth' in the fact of Frank's going to Italy, even if Aubyn were to allow it; and *I* would not, seeing how my gentleman behaved last night."

"You need not sneer at the poor lad, especially when his failings are the very things that make him an unconscious instrument ready to your hand."

"How? He *may* lose the papers, it is true; and the chances are that he will; but still there is a chance that he will not, which renders my 'way to power and wealth' a very probable blind alley."

"But he *must* and *shall* lose them!" was the quick retort of Emma. "Do you number no rogues among your best friends, who will not steal them for your sake, and the sake of a little money?"

"I had rather not trust another in the matter," he answered sulkily. "I had better go the errand myself, after all, if the deed be to be done."

You see there was a pretty clear understanding soon established between the two.

"Why, Denzil? What, are you mad? It will be hard work enough to make what we wish appear to be a natural event, under any circumstances; and yet you, on whom all suspicion would first rest, wish to put yourself in the most questionable position possible in connection with the matter."

"True," said Denzil; "I see that. But then consider the great danger of an accomplice. How he would have me in his power!"

"Is there no man of your acquaintance—the lower the better—over whom you hold something of this sort of power? It would, at least, put you on a more equal footing. Think, is there no one of whose secrets you know enough for this? Methinks there are sin and secrecy enough in the world to supply you."

"Yes," said Denzil, after a pause. "I have such a hold over Pentowan, the lawyer, down in the town."

"A lawyer!" said Emma. "Have you no other tool, less used to the devil's work, and therefore less likely to turn against the hand that wields it? But no matter—he is a coward; I have noticed it in his face often. But what is the power you hold over him? Let us make sure your title-deeds are better than Aubyn's." And again the smile came into Emma's face.

"Well, then, Nem," answered he, in that off-hand, slighting way, which a man adopts in repeating his peccadilloes to one of whose opinion of them he is not quite sure—"well, then, Nem, when I was in town with my father three years ago, while he was paying his addresses to one king, I paid mine to four—the respective monarchs of diamonds, hearts, clubs, and spades. Don't frown, child, I did not play deep—lost little, and won much!"

Emma had been brought up very strictly by Denzil's mother, who was very precise and stiff, almost puritanical in such matters, so that Emma had a disapproval of gambling that was not common in those days.

Denzil continued: "At the gaming-table I met Pentowan one night. He evidently knew no one, and, with his pompous vulgarity and familiar airs, was not making acquaintances. He therefore fixed on me with great glee, calling me 'Sir Denzil,' and was delighted to play with me, meaning, no doubt, to fleece me. I meant to fleece him, and my meaning was best, for I won two hundred guineas of him in half an hour's time. I was not too rich at the time, and so was willing to draw my winnings. I feigned an engagement as an excuse for leaving, and by way of a hint to him to pay. He gave me an I O U, which I declined, preferring the money, whereon he promised to bring me the cash next day. This he failed to do, but brought a bill purporting to be drawn by Sir Ashford Trekeye, a client of his. For lack of better I took this, whereupon he entreated me to keep it in my own hands for a week. His anxiety on the point aroused my doubts, and when he was gone I examined the paper, and came to the conclusion that, in consequence of my pressing him for the cash, he had forged this to keep me temporarily quiet while he raised the money.

"When he came to pay me, I taxed him with the forgery, and drawing for evidence a little on my imagination, I got the fat rascal to confess. So I forgave him the guineas and kept the paper, intending to make use of my goshawk, though to fly at much smaller game than I must now cast him off on."

"You have his neck in the noose, and taking all into consideration, I think we need have no fear but that he will serve our purpose. Remember, when the question of sending to Italy is mooted, you must express no opinion one way or the other."

"Very well! If you wish it; but Aubyn will think it strange."

"Hush!" interrupted Emma, "I hear Aubyn."

Denzil turned to go out of the window on to the lawn, but Emma threw herself in his way, whispering, as she put her arms round him, "Denzil, dearest, you know the meaning of this. A woman does not peril her soul, except for the man she loves. I must be your wife!"

CHAPTER VI.

VISITS OF CONDOLENCE.

WHEN Emma spoke the words with which the last chapter concluded, for a moment Denzil's brain swam. He had not seen this; in the thought of self he had forgotten to look for the reason of Emma's conduct. And then the little cottage under the limes came before him, and his wife's face flashed across his eyes.

So he gently unwound Emma's arms, and murmuring, "Yes, my wife—my wife!" he bent down to hide his face, and kissed her hand. Ah! that tiny hand; "all the perfumes of Arabia" cannot sweeten it, now that it has given the ratifying grasp in the evil compact! And so they parted for the present.

Denzil walked rapidly away from the house—almost ran. When he was out of sight, in a little plantation of firs, which maintained a precarious existence in spite of the wind, on the further side of the cliff, he flung himself down on the grass.

"By heaven, this is a difficult position! The

little witch took my breath away, positively! And how to evade her conditions I don't see—if I tell her I am married, I believe she would stab me.

"But there is time yet. First let me get Tresellan, and then the conditions she has made can be looked to afterwards. I was a fool not to see at once that she did not take the trouble to plan all this devilry without a selfish purpose. She always showed a preference for me over Aubyn, and my accursed vanity unhappily encouraged it. And yet not unhappily—for but for that I should never have had a chance of Tresellan. Apart from the fact that if she had not loved me she would have stood by her intended husband, I seriously believe that had she not suggested this scheme, and brought my regrets and fancies to grapple with it, in lieu of wasting themselves on the air, I should never have conceived the notion. By Jove, it's true that women are at the bottom of all evil. Why, this Nem has imagined, commenced even, this plot, without waiting for my consent or approval, and before I have had time to think."

And then this guilty man, satisfying his conscience by implicating another, fell to thinking of the heavy wrong he was about to do, and the reckoning he was preparing against his own soul. But the devil had a tight hold of his heart, and remorse was speedily silenced. So, after an hour's struggle between good and evil, in which the latter obtained an undoubted victory, Denzil returned to the house.

After Denzil's departure, Emma waited outside the window for Aubyn's arrival. But Aubyn stayed in the hall, for Frank, with red eyes and a pale face, and a tankard of ale in his hand, came in, looking rather ashamed.

"My dear Aubyn," he said, in a boisterous voice, which did not match his countenance, "I am delighted to see you looking so well. I owe you an apology for last night. I can't understand how it happened, for I have a tolerably good head."

"Don't say a word about it, Frank," answered Aubyn. "I confess I was sorry to see that you gave way to such a weakness—but let us say no more about it."

"I am glad to think, though, I am quite right to-day," responded the other, his eyes blinking woefully, and his under lip twitching all the while. "And so, coz, I am glad to be fit to offer my services to you. You know, Aubyn," and here he grew serious, "that I am ready to do anything in the world for you. As I have seen more of that same world than you have, my counsel and assistance will, I think, be of use to you. Command me—I am yours, heart and soul. If there is any office that needs especial care and prudence, such as only the deepest friendly affection can ensure—rely on me. Although a young man, I have enough experience to know what is needed in treating with the good folk who are supposed to form society. They are half of them rogues, and the other half fools—and I hardly know which are the most difficult to manage."

So spoke this budding philosopher. It is, I think, a sign of the clear-sightedness of youth, and a proof that age is blind, that young men should always be so quick to see the roguery and the folly of this stage, whereon we all take our parts. Young poets are always the melancholy ones, and old poets the cheerful ones. Young philosophers have the most determined opinions—and those, concerning the wickedness and sorrows of mankind; while the gray-beard sages are prone to be lenient to the human race, and give it credit for much goodness.

This is not odd. For, if it be true that men learn to forgive those faults in others which they themselves have committed, the elder folk have had the best opportunity of acquiring that self-born charity. The edge of sarcasm loses its keenness, when we find it must be turned to prune our own errors.

Frank's protestations and promises were not finished, when Lord Trenbrase, whose estate adjourned Tresellan, came into the hall.

"Sir Aubyn," said this nobleman, who had a portly and impressive appearance, "I have to apologize for intruding on you at such a moment. I was not aware that your father was dead when I came. I rode over, having heard of this wretched business, to inquire after him; and finding that all was over, I felt I could hardly leave without assuring you that I shall be most ready to render you any service that lies in my power. I respect you for yourself, my dear Sir Aubyn"—(he had seen him about six times)—"and cannot but feel glad that, since it was fated that we should lose poor Sir Abel, we shall have so worthy a successor in you. If it is not intruding unseasonably, I should much like to hear all you can tell me of the circumstances which led to your father's death. The ends of justice will be best attained by our tracking the murderers immediately; so you will, I know, pardon my thrusting this matter so unseemingly, as it must appear, before you now. Be assured my power shall be exerted to the utmost, and I think I may guarantee that before many days we shall have the guilty persons in our power."

Aubyn sat down with his lordship and gave him, as well as he could, the full particulars of the occurrence. The porter's son was called up, and my lord took copious notes of the boy's evidence. This occupied some time, and so it was but decent to ask him to stay and take a luncheon, which he did not refuse; and, the first restraint having worn off, a discussion with Frank on some question of military discipline (for the nobleman had been an officer in the army) kept Lord Trenbrase till about four o'clock in the afternoon.

As he mounted his horse, he promised Aubyn—and when I say promised, I mean volunteered with many binding oaths, such as garnished conversation in those days—to ride to Pengerrick at once, and communicate with the coastguard officer and the authorities.

But when he got to the cross-roads, and saw one arm of the sign-post pointing to Pengerrick, and the other to Trenbrase, my lord pulled up and hesitated, consulting his watch.

"Green, and Portune, and Sanders said they

would come and study the cards with me this evening, and there are those birds old Pollock sent me. Hang it, I can go to Pengerrick to-morrow. One day is of little importance, and I shall not get these jolly dogs together again in a hurry."

So my lord's gray hackney took the left-hand road, and my lord himself partook of old Pollock's birds, and gambled till early day with the three jolly dogs.

And next day came a headache, repentance, and good resolutions to set out to Pengerrick.

But my lord was low and ill, so he tried a hair of the dog that bit him, and then he tried another, and another, until he had taken the whole animal. The consequence was that he stayed at Portune's on his way to Pengerrick, and a bowl of punch and cards laid an embargo on him, and he returned to Trenbrase with all the necessaries for a headache, repentance, and good, but weak, resolutions for the next morning.

But why continue the tale of this nobleman's pavings of a place unmentionable with the very best of intentions? *Da capo!* It was not till after a week of alternate attempts and failures that he got to Pengerrick.

The customs officer did his best—and so did

everybody; that is to say, they shrugged their shoulders, called it an unhappy affair, and declaimed very loudly on it in company. But one and all expected somebody else to do the real work, so that the indignation they felt only served to set their tongues wagging, and no trace of the murderers was found.

Almost as soon as Lord Trenbrase left Tresellan, lawyer Pentowan presented himself. In his official capacity, there was no reason why he should not, so Aubyn received him. Our rosy-gilled man was overflowing with condolences and regrets. He loaded Aubyn with protestations of regard and respect, until the poor lad was almost ready to lay all the case before him.

But Emma, with feminine instinct, having divined this probability, prevented it by her presence, being determined that the lawyer should not be committed to Aubyn, and should first hear the circumstances from Denzil.

When the lawyer rose to go, Emma escorted him to the gateway. As they went, she looked round earnestly for Denzil, and she kept Pentowan talking for nearly an hour at the gate, in the hope that her cousin would come—but he did not make his appearance.

At last, as the lawyer was going, she said,

"Well, Mr. Pentowan, will you be found at your house to-morrow at three? Poor Aubyn is so distressed at present that he hardly knows what steps to take. By that time he will be more possessed, and, should he require your aid, will be grateful to you and me alike for having secured him this opportunity of consulting you."

So the rosy lawyer strode away, and Emma was left to her own reflections. They should not have been pleasant, but yet there was that inexplicable smile of hers on her face as she turned homeward.

I need not describe to you the family meeting that evening, when the project of the mission to Italy was discussed.

Lady Macbeth was full of wisdom. "Neither Aubyn nor Denzil must go. Frank, as the uninterested one, must undertake the task." Aubyn could not choose but be persuaded by this despotic little woman, and Denzil suffered all she did with wondering satisfaction.

As for Aunt Deborah, who had come from Devonshire in order to perform propriety, and take temporary command of the house, she was the devoutest believer in this affectionate little traitress. She bowed to her decisions in everything not connected with the household, over which she would insist on reigning supreme.

So the upshot was that Frank must go, and matters should stand as they were until his return.

"Denzil," whispered Lady Macbeth, as the council broke up, "Mr. Pentowan will be at home to-morrow at three. Be sure you see him!"

CHAPTER VII.

THE ECARTE OF INIQUITY.

CHRISTOPHER PENTOWAN'S office was a gloomy place, well fitted for the dark work that was done there. The two windows were so grimed with the dirt of years that they toned down the daylight to dusk. The showers of many winters had left their traces on the grimy panes in tortuous watercourses, typical of law, and looking as if at night ghosts of long-buried clients crowded round the windows, and pressing their faces close to the glass to gaze in at the scene of their ruin, had left these marks of their tears.

Three or four gnats kept up a soft music, and a strayed reveller, in the shape of a bluebottle from the grocer's over the way, took an occasional noisy career round the room, terminating with a bang as he brought-to against the dirty panes aforesaid. Dusty cobwebs there were many, where great hairy spiders sat looking out for clients.

The whole scene appeared like the opening of

a pantomime. Do not pantomimes, as a rule, commence in gloom? Tingle! tingle! goes the prompter's bell, and the gasman turns down the footlights and dims the chandelier. Then, to the low thrilling strains of the orchestra the curtain rises on a dark cloud in Fairydom, or a darker dungeon on earth, or a darkest cavern under the earth, wherein strange demons are flapping about on various errands.

In the dim, but scarcely religious, light of Pentowan's office, there was only one familiar to be seen. He was seated at a high desk, driving a strident quill that added its discordant notes to the trumpets of the gnats and the drone-pipe of the bluebottle "aforesaid." You see, I am legal, to be in keeping with the scene.

This familiar was Christopher's clerk, Gregory Williams, a man somewhat past the middle age, but one who, owing to the preservative influence of an eccentric character, carried into his later years much of the spirit of his youth.

At this precise moment, however, he was depressed in mind, for he had been roused by the intermittent bluebottle to organize a pursuit of it, which ended in the breaking of one of the windows. Gregory had concealed the breach with a ledger, but he knew that it would some time or other be perceived. Then would follow a deduction from his meagre salary, which was barely sufficient to allow him his one luxury, an occasional modest glass and pipe in the sanded parlour of the "Ship" with the Rev. Mr. Sterrup.

Gregory Williams, who was the son of a small chemist and grocer in Plymouth, had attached himself to the fortunes of Pentowan as an errand-boy, and had gradually grown up into the full-fledged clerk and confidential man. He was as honest as the day, and full of kindness and goodness. How it happened that he was where he was, heaven only knows! He was troubled with doubts at times when he had to carry out some extra sharp practice; but, on the whole, he believed in the incomprehensible goodness of the law, and though he half regretted his choice of a profession on occasions, he fancied it all worked round to good. As for his master's villany, he never suspected that, though Pentowan took little care to hide it from him. Pentowan's line of conduct towards him was thoroughly in accordance with his class of mind. Wicked himself, he thought everybody else about him wicked until he had established them otherwise. At first he suspected Gregory; tried, and re-tried, tempted, and proved him. Then, finding that the clerk came out unscathed; in fact, was an honest man, he immediately had the greatest confidence in, and contempt for, him. Once satisfied on this point, he set him down as a fool, that being, in his opinion, identical with an honest man.

And here see the blindness of evil-doing! For it was this honest clerk who eventually brought Christopher's card-house about his ears. In future, rogues all, don't have too great a faith in the folly of honest folk, and so save your necks from the halter—for, upon my word, I am loath to see even you hanged.

Well, as I have said, for the reason just alleged, Pentowan took no pains to conceal his rascality from Gregory, who, perhaps, from the very openness of the evil suspected nothing. You get your pocket picked by the man who stands in front of you, looks in your face, and quietly transfers your property to himself. But you are tolerably likely to catch, or be on your guard against, the fellow who creeps up behind you, or sidles towards you with restless glances.

Nevertheless there was a sort of lurking doubt at the bottom of Gregory's heart that never went quite to sleep, and indeed became really troublesome at times when the evening was wearing late at the "Ship," and the "Hollands" growing low.

The very dingy old timepiece behind the door was pointing close upon three when Christopher entered the office—for, if punctuality could confer respectability, Pentowan was the most respectable of rascals. And the clock had not long struck three when he was called away to speak to Denzil. Another punctual rascal. Upon my word, I believe honesty to be much less business-like and regular than knavery. In fact, villany has to attend to these things, and wrap all the rags and shreds of propriety it can find about it—while virtue is far too careless on these points. Make it a rule of life, reader mine, to have your doubts of a punctual man.

When Denzil came to the house, Lucinda made her escape into the garden, for she hated one brother as much as she admired the other. She was a woman of decision and strong feeling, and where she disliked, disliked with a purpose. She was one of those people who, when they would say they disapprove of a thing, say they hate it. And they are not the less worthy for having "thorough" minds, I fancy.

But Pentowan, who read in Denzil's face (for our second rogue was not that perfect rogue, a hypocrite, just yet) that he had important matters to talk over, was not content with the privacy of the sitting room. He led the way to the office, whence he soon despatched Williams, on heaven only knows what mission of roguery, in order that they might have the place entirely to themselves.

Then our two gentlemen sat down to cards—not the actual "devil's books"—but those metaphorical ones that sharpers use in their dealings with one another.

It was not long before Denzil showed his hand to the lawyer, who was far too well versed in all the combinations of the pack in use among bad men, not to see what the younger player wanted.

"I see, sir! The link in the chain of evidence once dropped, your claim to the estate is indisputable. The certification of the marriage! It is but a perishable bit of paper between you and the broad acres. But how to get rid of it?"

"It *must* be got rid of, Mr. Pentowan," said Denzil fiercely. "If once I have it in my possession, the fire will soon have little but ashes to show for it. Tinder tells no tales. And listen! If *you* procure it for me, the same flame that destroys it shall consume a certain bill that you and I know of. I think that perishable bit of paper must come between you and your comfort scores of times."

Christopher's jolly face grew very white, and he showed most unmistakable signs of astonishment. In truth, he had not calculated on Denzil's keeping the forged document, and, up to this moment, had been calculating on payment for any services he did in the business which Denzil was planning out to him. It was a disappointment to find that they would only be regarded as a set-off.

"Bungler's luck"—the first trick to score to the younger player.

But Christopher had not been doing the devil's work so many years for that potentate to desert him altogether. So he was able with a tolerably calm face and voice to ask—

"And pray how can *I* assist?"

"By following Frank Rewth to Italy—nay, preceding him, if possible—and obtaining the papers from the priest."

"Nay, nay, Mr. Denzil. Consider my professional duties here—my time—the expense—the danger."

"Pshaw! the expense I will fore-arm you against; the time I will pay for to thrice the amount of the bill I have in my desk signed by you in some one else's name; the danger is little,—less than you have set at nought often before now. And the professional engagements will be not so much interfered with as they would be, were I to hand you and the forgery over to the governor of Bodmin prison."

"I am not afraid of your threats, Mr. Denzil," said Christopher; though he was, the coward, all the time. "But I will do what I can in the matter for you."

"Here's my hand," said Denzil, and he mentally scored the second trick to himself. Yet our Greek was only finessing, and had a good card in his hand yet. But he was not going to show it until he had seen all his adversary's game. So they shook hands—each thinking he had the odd trick in his favour;—and there was no honour to count on either side.

It only remained to arrange the plan of Christopher's going. He and Denzil sat down, for they had been pacing the office to and fro before, and chatted over their rascality as if they had been accomplices in crime for years.

There is a sort of freemasonry in every habit, virtuous or vicious. When you get into a railway carriage, you may travel from London to Edinburgh without exchanging a word with your travelling companion. But, take out your cigar-case and ask if he objects to smoking, and you will soon be puffing away on the most confidential terms, having discovered that you have scores of mutual friends, and are, perhaps, even distantly connected. The community of habit makes you intimate in spite of British reserve.

Thus it was that Denzil and Christopher were laying their heads together in so unreserved and friendly a manner; letting out their evil designs and black thoughts to each other with as little restraint as if they had been a brace of philanthropists planning a benevolent institution.

Faugh! I declare the atmosphere of this den of iniquity stifles me. Let us get out into the garden. There we shall no doubt find Lucinda training the yellow rose over the arbour, or clearing the dead leaves from the jessamine on the porch.

Let us take a turn down between the yew-hedges into the bleaching lawn; she may be there feeding the peacock; or she may be watching the bees against the south wall, or the pigeons by the stable. Not there either! Where can she be? Let us stroll down toward the office-window.

CHAPTER VIII.

A LISTENER WHO HEARS EVIL.

What woman is this, with wild eyes and white lips, standing beneath the window of Pentowan's office? Lucinda. And well may she look pale and terrified! As she leant over the violets which she had planted among the lilies of the valley in this quiet corner, where there was a nook of shade all day long, she heard something of the tale which Denzil was telling. Interested, she hardly knew why, in all that concerned Aubyn, and forgetting for the moment that she was eaves-dropping, she listened until her interest grew into surprise—her surprise into doubt—her doubt into horror. Was it the real wind that fanned her cheek? was it the real odour of violets that it brought to her; were the trees real whose whispers mingled with the low voices? was the sky real? or was she only dreaming?

It seemed barely possible that Aubyn's brother should be plotting against him, and that the instrument chosen to plot his ruin was her own father! Oh! Gregory, Gregory, when that random ruler broke the pane, you called the bluebottle a demon! Surely it was a winged thing more like a good angel. But for that fracture Lucinda might have gathered her violets, and Denzil might have gathered the fruits of his iniquity; for the window-panes were whitened over inside, and the conspirators spoke very low. But that most providential fly altered all that this chronicle would else have had to relate. Only see what mice of chance may let loose lions of circumstance.

You must keep my portrait of Lucinda in your mind all this time. She was too majestic a creature to shiver, and quail, and exhaust all her energy in crying.

She stood like a statue, with her white lips apart, fixed, and apparently lifeless, but, in reality, with all her senses on the alert. The life, driven back to her heart, rallied there, and stood at bay fiercely. You might, perhaps, have run needles into her flesh without her wincing; but no word or slightest movement of yours would have escaped that vigilant sentinel, the brain. One of your little women—even Emma Rewth—would have fainted or screamed; but she did neither. Her mind, which, like her hand, could be meted by no six and a half mental measure, grasped the whole case at once, and though physically unnerved, she only paid that much tribute to womanly nature, and rose in intellect above the weakness of her sex.

When the interview was over, and Denzil had left, and Christopher had closed the door on him, Lucinda seemed to wake from her reverie. With a firm step she passed up the garden, between the yew-hedges out into the bleaching lawn.

At the further end of this was a cedar, under the low-hanging boughs of which she had been accustomed to shelter when as a child she was crossed or vexed; for this queenly lady had been a most imperious little person when young. Thither she now mechanically bent her steps, and in its sombre shade sat for at least an hour, meditating the best course to be adopted.

The first idea which presented itself was to appeal to her father's better feelings. But the discovery of evil in one whom she had hitherto so utterly relied upon, led her to judge with extreme severity. It is not unnatural that, where we have confided too much, we should distrust too much when we find we have been deceived. Nor is this true only of the individual, it holds good in the case of communities. When once the world discovers that a well-to-do usurer has committed a murderous assault on a man who had never injured him, it before long begins to persuade itself that the murderous weapons have been similarly employed before, and rakes up from its memory, or its invention, the story of two or three bodies mysteriously found in the Thames, showing evidences of having been pistolled. Nay, it even goes so far as to hint at some connection between the miserable money-lender and the strange carpet-bag and its horrible contents found at Waterloo Bridge.

The great difficulty which Lucinda found arose from the lingering sense of duty and affection which, in spite of mistrust such as I have described, would fain shield her father from the consequences of her revealing the plot to Aubyn. His easy good nature, too incredulous, would have put aside her cautions as unnecessary, her hints as unjustifiable. Perhaps her heart misgave her, and she dreaded lest, where, as yet, she did not think she had made any impression, she might begin by creating a bad one.

At last she hit on a plan.

About ten minutes after Gregory's return from the errand on which Pentowan had sent him, the ledger, with which he had so carefully concealed the breach in the window, was pushed aside, and a quiet voice, that made the poor clerk spring off his high stool with surprise, begged him to come at once into the garden.

Such an act was infinitely more bold than anything poor Gregory could muster courage to do, so he thrust his lank visage up against the broken pane and protested—

"But Miss Lucinda——"

"Then open the window," was all the answer he got.

So the sash was raised, and Lucinda began her story.

"Gregory," said she, laying her dainty palms on the two inky paws that rested on the window-sill, "you have been so kind to me since I was a child—you have carried me about to the shows, and led me along the beach so often, that I feel you will be good to me now, when I want some one to be good to me—oh! so much."

There was a wonderful look of tenderness in the rugged old face as it looked down on the ripe, blooming one beneath it. Williams had known Lucinda as a baby, had been her playmate, and almost nurse—so no wonder she trusted to his faithfulness.

"Gregory, my father is a wicked man!"

"Oh! no, no, miss; a lawyer. We don't understand the law, you and I; but, as he often explains to me, the law is the result of careful deliberation and much trouble, on the part of those infinitely wiser than us; and if it seems at times to work ill, it is only because we cannot see the ultimate good it will do, and" (here Gregory came down to his natural tone, for, to say the truth, he had been quoting Christopher for the last sentence or so, word for word)—"and I confess it *is* hard to see it at times."

"It is not the law that is to blame now, Gregory. What does the law say to people who destroy documents belonging to others?"

"Felony, madam; flat felony. I can refer to the books at once."

"Hush! there is no necessity for that. But there *is* necessity for immediate action—and silence, Gregory."

And ere long Gregory was in possession of the Tresellan history, and the schemes of Denzil and his master. To describe his state of mind, when first he realized all this, would be to attempt a theme, which even Moses eschewed, namely, chaos.

But Lucinda was not contented to stop until she had got his brains into some sort of order, and had impressed upon them the course of action on which she had decided. This was, that Williams was to follow or accompany her father as might be managed best; that he was never to leave him; and when they fell in with Frank Rewth, to keep watch and ward over him and his trust. She knew sufficient of poor Frank's failings—notorious enough in Polvadnick—to be aware how necessary such a guardianship would be.

I don't know that such very clever people as you or I, good reader, would have entrusted so delicate a business to old Gregory, taciturn, simple soul that he was; but Lucinda had long known and respected him, and possibly discerned the good that was in him through the ungainly crust, just as a naturalist discerns a brilliant and swift gauze-winged fly, in what you and I should call a slothful, brown water-monster. Some characters remain in the larva state all their lives for want of the right temperature to develop them. Gregory's was not fated to be one of them.

In the evening, Christopher informed Lucinda that he was obliged to go to France on important business. Had she never been near the broken pane, this might have pass unnoticed, for there was some sort of business that frequently took our worthy lawyer to the opposite coast. He never said what the exact nature of these foreign transactions was, but I have a shrewd guess it had more to do with silk and lace than with parchment and ferret.

But Lucinda was not prepared to let him go very easily.

"*Must* you go, father? I feel a presentiment of mischance and evil: and this afternoon as I was in the garden, the feeling was so strong I could not help hoping you would not be going from home just now."

I don't think Christopher felt too comfortable, bad as he was, to hear of his daughter's presentiments; for, mind you, your wicked man, who does not fear God, often fears the devil in most superstitious fashion, and will quake if a magpie cross his path, or an old woman shake her beard at him. Lucinda saw the feeling, and was not displeased, attributing it to a twinge of conscience instead of a spasm of selfish fear. Still he protested that he must go. She begged of him to take Gregory with him, but to this Christopher could not consent. But she was so urgent, that at last he was obliged to yield, inwardly resolved that he would somehow contrive to dispense with the clerk at the last moment.

And so, having promised this, he kissed his daughter and bade her good night; for the moon was high in heaven now, dappling the little bay with silvery light. One by one the lights in the houses disappeared, and darkness wrapt the town in its misty embrace, save where, here and there, some late fisher was mending his nets, or a taper was burning in a sick room. The noise of the corn-crake was the only sound that mingled with the lapping of the tide, as in the dead of night it crept up the shingle, sparkled against the sea-wall in myriads of phosphorescent points, and then stole back again before the first long rays of morning lit up the topmost turret of Tresellan.

That night, quiet, and dark, and slumbrous, as the little town appeared, there were many heads tossing on restless pillows in it. Frank Rewth was leaning half out of his window looking over the waters he was to cross on the morrow, and furtively smoking a pipe of Virginia to the accompaniment of a tankard of spiced claret that his good friend the housekeeper had compounded for him with her own hands. He was long before he sought his couch.

Emma was lying quite still with closed eyes, but with all her soul in tumult; and Denzil was plunging in alternate waking and dozing fits, that were equally tormenting with sleeping fantasies and waking fancies.

Gregory was stretched on his humble pallet, which became a rack for the nonce. He felt that hitherto he had been treading the path of destruction in his blind obedience to his master, but that he had still a chance of safety—to be reached only by an arduous struggle. His reflections were hopeful, but painful. It was something like the agony of being revived after drowning.

Poor Lucinda's were the most terrible hours of vigil. The strain over—the difficulty seen and guarded against, as far as possible—the crisis past,—her feelings flowed back in their old channels—her artificial strength left her natural weakness over-taxed; and when she remembered her father and his crimes, it is no wonder that the tears flowed and flowed until her very heart seemed melting in that long fit of weeping, not passionate, but irresistible and terrible from its very quiet. For the tears overflowed as if from the overcharged bosom, calmly and incessantly, and unbroken by sobs. The utter prostration of such grief was dreadful beyond words. Meantime the father, for whom she was suffering all this undeserved agony, was sleeping as people tell us only good consciences can sleep. But it was not a quiet mind that was accountable for this heavy slumber.

When Christopher retired to rest he opened a little drawer of the cabinet in the recess between the windows, and took a small bottle from it. A few drops were poured into a glass (which was afterwards very carefully washed by him) and tossed off. A faint odour of poppy was diffused through the room. In that drawer were many other little bottles, carefully stoppered and labelled in cypher. It seems Christopher had his own pharmacopœia, and did not put his trust in the Polvadnick doctors.

CHAPTER IX.

A SLIPPERY CUSTOMER.

It was an angry morning. The clouds were ragged and jagged, blown about a red sky. The sea was tumbling in upon the beach in hoarse breakers, and all the boats in the bay were tossing wildly. Not one was loosed from its moorings, for, as the fishers' saying ran—"A dry hand with no money in it was better than a dead wet one full of sand."

In a word, there was a storm brewing. When Christopher came to the beach it was long before he could get a fisherman to put to sea with him. His plan was to sail for the coast of France, from whence he could get overland to Piedmont, if he did not meet with a Mediterranean vessel in mid-channel.

One after another the boatmen declined, in spite of the tempting gold he displayed. At last old Simon—Gibbet Simon, as he was called—undertook, for a heavy sum, to put him on board a vessel if one were to be met with, for he declined the idea of approaching the French shore with the wind in the quarter in which it lay.

So the boat was hauled down from the high point where it had been beached in the morning, and they were just about to set off for the fishing-smack, which was moored among the tiny fleet in the bay, when Christopher, with a well-acted astonishment, turned to Gregory—

"I protest I have left my purse on the table in my bed-room. Stop, Simon! And you, Gregory, run and fetch it for me."

What a shallow artifice! as Gregory might have seen if he had but paused. For where was the need of the purse to a gentleman who had pockets full of guineas to tempt the boatmen withal? But Williams was hardly out of the fog which had bewildered his senses all night, and so he instinctively obeyed his master. And no sooner was the worthy clerk lost from sight, than Christopher, shouting to Simon to help, pushed the boat off with a skill that betrayed some knowledge of things nautical, and long before Gregory had reached Pentowan's door, the boat was alongside the smack.

"Cut the mooring—there's a guinea to pay for the rope," said Christopher, as, in a very sailorly manner, he began to get the jib clear; and before long the light craft was skimming out among the hissing crests of the waves, now rising, now plunging head downwards in the broken sea, and driving on toward the blue-gray storm-clouds that were laboriously climbing up the sky in the teeth of the wind.

Lucinda was sitting in the room under Christopher's, when she heard the clerk blunder up the stairs, and begin bustling about overhead.

"What! not sailed, Gregory?" she exclaimed, as she ran into the room, to find him like a bewildered owl, plunging here and there, peeping into a bottle, or opening a box in vain search.

"No, madam; the purse—left on the table" —(here he peeped with one curious eye into an Eau de Cologne flask, as if any purse available for foreign travel could ever have been bestowed there)—"and the master's waiting."

"But you must have delayed on the beach; you left the house full an hour ago."

"Yes; but the fishermen won't put out, miss," said Gregory, stopping, with a woe-begone face, and sitting down in a chair to recover his breath. "Your father's had to make the guineas fly, I'll warrant, before he could get one to go to sea. And that one is Gallows Simon, who—Lord forgive me!—is not meant to be drowned if the mark on his neck means anything."

"Why, Gregory, Gregory, are you asleep?" said Lucinda, shaking him. "What does my father need a purse for, if he has guineas to give to boatmen so lavishly? Why, he has been deceiving you, Gregory!"

I think Gregory began to see it by this time, for his visage lengthened in wonderful fashion, as he began to make a speech, about which we shall never be able to discover whether it was intended as an apology or an explanation, for before his lips had formed the first word, Lucinda was gone.

While Williams was recovering from his wonderment at her sudden disappearance he heard her calling him, and following the voice, mounted to an upper room, whence from a window in the roof they could command a view of the bay. Lucinda pointed to a red sail that a stray watery sunbeam flecked brightly, as it stood in relief against the gray castellated cloud, still climbing up slowly in the teeth of the wind.

"That boat is the one that carries my father."

"There is no boat out fishing to-day; you are right, Miss Lucinda. And now what is to be done? What a fool—what a dolt to be so easily deceived!"

If they could have seen so far, they might have noted a very satisfied smile on the face of Christopher as he stood with his arm round the little mizen-mast of the smack, and saw that no boat was setting out in pursuit—for he had half feared that his dogged, faithful old clerk would follow him. You may smile, Master Kit! But the worst day's work you ever did for yourself you have just accomplished. "It's the last straw that breaks the horse's back," says the old saw. That conviction of wrong-doing, that all Lucinda's arguments and proofs had failed to produce satisfactorily in Gregory's mind, was born at once of the knowledge of this last deception. I don't think that from that moment the old clerk failed to see an evil design in every word and action of his master's. And, when Christopher had so suspicious a watcher, how could he fail to be detected?

The two gazers at the window stayed long with their eyes fixed on the distant boat. But their thoughts were busy all the while. Meantime, the smack laboured through the livid troughs of the waves, that struck her trembling timbers furiously as she heaved and rolled before the fitful gusts, which now strained every rope and bellied out the russet-sail, and anon dropped suddenly, leaving it shivering and flapping as the boat drifted at random, or, veering for a moment, drove the canvas a-back against the creaking mast, while the hoarse, hissing waves tumbled in over the stern, threatening to overwhelm the frail bark.

Presently a curtain of rain descended between the watchers and the boat; it came nearer and nearer; the sand on the shore turned from white to brown; the roofs glistened and darkened; and, in another second, the fierce torrent was pattering at the window that Lucinda had hastily closed.

A swift darkness spread over the scene, and it was not without difficulty that Gregory crept down the narrow stair leading from the garret: a portion of the house with which he had never before been acquainted.

He was too busily engaged while there, or he might have noticed several bales and bundles stowed away in its darkest corner.

When they reached the lower rooms, Lucinda made the old clerk sit down, and with a shrewdness that would have delighted her father (had it been displayed for any other purpose than this particular one), managed to glean all the information he had to give about her father's course.

She saw that it was just possible for Gregory

to overtake him before he got to Terini (the village where Father Seraphicus resided), if Gregory, amply supplied with money, travelled overland. Her father would be delayed by Simon's objections to a lee shore, or some time possibly in the channel.

"You must start by daybreak to-morrow, provided the weather be fine, and hire a boat to put you on shore at St. Elu; once there, I must leave it to you to get on to Piedmont; but, remember, there must be no sparing of money; thrift, in the matter of a few guineas, may be the cause of misery—nay, death."

"But permit me, Miss Lucinda," said Gregory, in whose face Lucinda had noted a growing difficulty; "how am I to be supposed to know that Mr. Pentowan is gone to this place—Terini?" and Gregory appealed to the paper of names which Lucinda had written to aid him on his route.

"True, I had forgot that."

Here was a difficulty very hard of solution. If they had not known where he was going, they could not have been further from their object.

But what all their scheming could not effect, the interposition which human beings call Chance brought about for them.

When the storm had passed over Polvadnick and was roaring up the gorges on the moorland to the north, setting the great echoes flapping among the rocks like dragons startled from their slumbers, Denzil, whose uneasy conscience left him no rest, came down into the town to see if Christopher had started.

He was ushered into the room where Lucinda was seated. His inquiries were sufficiently unguarded (and not unnaturally so, for how was he to dream of that listener under the broken pane?) to warrant Lucinda's question—

"Oh! then you know where my father is gone? I am so glad, for he sent back Gregory for some money, and other important matters; and, before we could find them, the boatman, who was hardly to be prevailed on to go at all, hurried off, fearful of the late storm, and, in order to intercept an outward-bound ship, which was discovered to eastward. Gregory had special orders to follow him at any cost; but he is a slow and not overbright man, however excellent a clerk; and so, though prepared to follow his master anywhere, he is quite at a loss now in what direction to look for him. Can you assist me?"

Denzil looked hard at Lucinda, but her brown eyes were too grand to be stared out of their secret easily. It would never do, he thought, to refuse; it would seem suspicious, perhaps, hereafter—and it is possible Christopher has need of the money or whatever it is.

Lucinda appeared not to observe the delay involved in this train of thought; indeed, the delay was not long.

"He will pass through Terini, a small place in the north of Italy. That is the extent of my knowledge of his movements, for he has a commission to perform for me hard by there."

"It is a small clue," said Lucinda, "but better than none; so I thank you."

Denzil took his departure in an uncomfortable state of mind. He did not see how he could have avoided giving thus much information; indeed, to retain it might, by delaying Pentowan, upset his own plans. And yet it had been better had the name of that Italian village never passed his lips; for who could tell what might not be talked of when he ousted Aubyn from the heirship?

He must consult with Emma. Accordingly, he went home immediately, to find that young lady engaged in arranging, with her own hands, the valise that was to be our dandy Frank's travelling companion.

When he had finished his story, Nem sprang up with a troubled face, and began to pace the room with a quick step, her little hands clasped behind her and her eyes bent on the ground.

"Denzil, there's something wrong here. Can the father have told her, or does she suspect?"

"Why, Nem, what do you dream about? She only asked if I knew where her father was going, which, considering that I was there yesterday, and again to-day to ask whether he had left, was not very unreasonable,—for a woman! No, what troubles me is not what she knows or thinks now, but what may enter her mind by and by, when certain circumstances occur, under which it is possible that a certain Padre Serafico of Terini may come to be publicly spoken of."

"True, very true," said Emma; "and yet it seemed—ah! well, it is possible conscience makes us cowardly."

"But what do you think? Is there harm done?"

"If done, it is done. It is past mending; for it would not better matters were you to go to this woman and ask her as a favour not to think any more about Terini. You said a rude thing about women just now, which was untrue; but this is true, that if you tell a woman to forget anything, it is only a stronger incentive to her remembering it."

She returned to her task, but the thought of Lucinda still seemed to prey on her mind; for, as she was fixing the last buckle of the valise, she said—

"But, at all events, I will go and see her. I will read her heart, and you shall know what she thinks."

Emma rather prided herself on reading characters and thoughts at a glance, which she could do to some extent. It is a faculty that no one I ever met with has been possessed of, but which almost everybody I have met with fancied they possessed. It is, perhaps, as well that Heaven is sparing of an endowment so terrible. These people, with a self-satisfied smirk, tell us they can look into others' souls, and read what is written there. Could they read even their own, the record would be sufficiently awful to banish smiles from their faces for ever. Poor children! we look at mirrors whose surfaces reflect ourselves, and cry out, "Into what depths our searching eyes penetrate!"

CHAPTER X.

A PARTING AND A MEETING.

It was late in the day ere Frank was ready to start for Plymouth, where it was arranged that he was to take a ship for Marseilles, from which port he could easily get to his final destination in a coasting felucca.

The two servants, who were to accompany him as guards, were in saddle already. At that time none of the gentry ever attempted the journey across Brand Down—or Brandon, as it is now called—without a retinue, for there were plenty of footpads about, whose trade it was to stop rich merchants going to and from Falmouth.

Frank handed his valise to a groom, and then hastened upstairs to take a last look at the uncle who had been a second father to him. He was grieved to think that he must go without paying the last sad duty of following his benefactor's body to the grave. But that was not to be.

The impatience of Emma, who seemed to wish

to hasten on the accomplishment of the guilt she contemplated, was the cause of this. With a thousand plausible reasons she impressed on Aubyn the necessity of setting all doubts of his birth at rest before the time of mourning was over, so that when he again went into the world, as master of Tresellan, he might have his title clear for all to read.

Frank leaned over the corpse, and pressed a kiss on its cold lips, leaving a tear on its calm forehead. I fear Frank's tears were womanly tears—easily set flowing, and with springs nearer to the eyes than the heart is. Though he passed out of the house with a grave, sad face, and rode solemnly away, the shadow of the dark valley did not pursue him long.

As his horse began to warm to its stride across the open moor, the fresh air, rich with the breath of the furze and heather, and setting the blood a-tingle with the brine of the neighbouring ocean, blew on his cheek and tossed his brown curls about. The startled birds sprang out of the bushes and darted away, rising and sinking by turns in their flight in front, as if to invite his steed to race with them. Flocks of larks, mounting high to take a last look at the sun, flickered, alternate sparkles and spots, far up in the blue, while their notes rained down, filling the air with song.

What power can Death have over so young a heart—a heart full of life, and hope, and buoyancy? Let us not blame poor Frank if presently he bursts into a song, as his horse bears him easily along in its swinging gallop over the elastic turf. As he rode into the streets of Plymouth, the bugles were ringing out their last summons, and here and there disorderly troopers were clattering along the streets towards barracks. Frank recognized the uniform—it was the regiment he was to have joined—so that he was not much astonished when, on turning a corner, he almost rushed into the arms of the cornet, his quondam adversary in the duel of which I have spoken.

At that period of English history when my men and women were alive, and not mere characters in a novel, opponents in a duel shook hands and were the dearest friends after having fiercely sought one another's lives ten minutes before. Frank and the cornet did not disgrace their times—they were sworn comrades, and bore no malice. It is more than possible that when there are only two rapiers—or twenty paces and a brace of bullets—between you and another, that you are gifted for the nonce with a portion of that penetration, of which, in a single chapter back, I said so many people believed themselves, and so few really were, possessed. At all events, the strongest friendships, and the profoundest mutual respect and admiration, grew out of these murderous encounters; and if you did not kill your opponent, or he you, the chances were you would be ready to lay down your lives for each other ever after. All this, if you please, I plead as a palliation for Frank's yielding to the urgent request of his friend to come to his quarters, and drink a tankard of claret in memory of old times. "Boats for Marseilles! Why, the Sound was full of them. Frank would have no difficulty in procuring one in the morning." And perhaps he would not, if he had tried: but truth to tell, he was in bed groaning with a splitting headache, and the consciousness of having lost all his money at cards to the garrison chaplain, who, if he had studied holy writ as closely as he had studied the "devil's books," would have had all the texts in it at his fingers' ends. Headache, repentance, and empty pockets: it's an old story, and comes down to our time with a "to be continued" at the end of it.

The headache was not very difficult of cure.

The homœopathic prescription of spiced ale and toast soon proved effectual. The repentance disappeared with the last throbbing of the temples. But the empty pockets were not so easily remedied. So between the getting of these evils, and the getting rid of them, our well-intentioned lad lost two days. "Well-intentioned!" It's the very saddest epitaph you could write on anybody's tomb. There's no creature in this world that does more harm, and suffers more for doing it, than these poor paviours of a place not to be spoken of.

Let us now turn back a bit, and find out what became of Christopher after the curtain of rain descended between him and the gazers from the window.

Neither he nor Gibbet Simon had contemplated such a storm as descended upon them, or they would not have sailed. The wind was one continuous blast, not spent in sudden gusts, but pressing a dead weight on the little vessel, as if to crush it into the boiling waters. The sail was soon struck; but, small as the surface the boat presented then, it was driven on with as much speed as if every stitch of canvas was set. Simon clung to the tiller with a pertinacity that was born of instinct rather than reason, and turned the head as well as might be to meet the force of the waves. The lightning showed both faces pale with terror. Christopher formed ever so many good resolutions, and sketched out a career of brilliant repentance for himself. But resolutions and repentance faded in the daylight that followed the tempest. For at last the rage of the elements was spent, and the dripping boat tossed on the yet restless billows, in the cold sunbeams that streamed pale through the humid atmosphere.

About half a mile to eastward a foreign-built brig was making her way down channel. She must have taken refuge betimes, in some snug haven, from the violence of the storm, for her white canvas had never been ruffled, and every rope and shroud was in its place, seen quite clearly through the intervening air, rendered more pellucid than ever by the presence of water.

Before long the boat was laid-to under the quarter of the stranger, and Christopher, who learnt she was bound for Gibraltar, stepped on board. Then Simon turned his boat's head homeward, spread her brown wings to the wind, and before evening her keel was grating on the Polvadnick beach.

Simon had been nick-named Gibbet by his rough mates in consequence of a red mark round his neck, and many were the rude jests made at his expense when he was seen setting off with Christopher—"he need not fear water who was to die with his feet in his boots and their soles off the ground."

But it was scrofula, not Fate, that had so marked Simon; and he died at last in his own little hut, on his hard pallet-bed, with his wife and children weeping round him. But to that day of his death he kept a solemn vow he had made on this occasion, "that never, by night or day, fair or foul, would he take a lawyer in his boat further from shore than the length of a good swim."

The lower classes knew more of Christopher than the squirearchy; and the whispers of his hard dealings, though loud enough at the "Ship," never got so far even as the kitchen at Tresellan. But, despite his good character with well-to-do-folks, Pentowan was known, feared, and hated by the poor. No wonder, then, that once or twice a thought crossed the mind of poor Simon during that storm which would not have allowed our lawyer to rest quite so comfortably as he did even then, wrapt in his cloak in the bottom of the boat. This fleeting notion was no other than to cast the man of sin overboard, and thus lighten the boat of what he feared was likely to lead to its foundering. The putting into execution of this design would have lightened the toils of the present historian, but would have been mighty unpleasant to Christopher, for there was not even a dog-fish alongside at the time; and I doubt whether the shark I once hooked myself, a little way from the Eddystone, would have had a sufficiently capacious maw for such a portly Jonah.

Christopher, once on board the Spanish trader, had a fine run to Gibraltar, and got on thence by a coaster to Italy.

Frank, also, made his journey—when at length he did start—under favourable circumstances.

Gregory, too, reached the coast of France in safety. His funds were supplied by his master's strong cash-box, which Lucinda soon compelled to disgorge its contents—though the persuasion needed was so strong even as a hammer. This, wielded by that round arm of hers, which a sculptor would have chosen as a model for Diana rather than Aphrodite, soon overcame all scruples, and the fat guineas tumbled out on the office table in tolerable plenty.

So now, if you please, we will leave these three competitors in this important race to struggle on by land and sea to their goal. Who is to be first—who is to win? Virtue is as often the hare as the tortoise, in this notably contradictory world of ours.

The same evening that Frank left Tresellan, Emma strolled over to the cliffs above Osprey Lodge, as Christopher had designated his cottage.

As she neared a corner of the road, the declining red sun lighting up her face, she was aware of a long shadow that told of some one's approach to the turn. Two more steps, and Lucinda and Emma were face to face.

It was their first meeting; for Emma seldom came to the eastern side of the town, and Lucinda was, like your tall queenly brunettes, somewhat indolent, and a stay-at-home.

The path sloped toward the town. If this story were to be illustrated by a single frontispiece, this is the scene I should select for it. Emma's path lies downward, Lucinda's up—types of their fates; their eyes were thus on a level, and each gazed on the other as fixedly and long as only women can do. Emma's hair—in the picture I imagine—should flutter out seaward with those tantalizing curls that Julian Portch can draw so enchantingly; and her dress should float about one of Leech's dainty boots, and she should have eyes born of Hablot Browne's pencil, and lips rounded by Kenny Meadows; and Millais should give the folds in her dress, the breaks in her silk mantle—or Watson or Walker should draw the whole. It would be very pretty with the rich sunset-light poured over it. But what about Lucinda—her face in the shade, with the red sky behind her? Majestic as her figure is, the mere outline would not convey her to the mind. She was one of those women who want colour to make their likenesses true—and, with all her grand face and form, there was a softness and delicacy about her features—and a character, moreover, that no draughtsman work could represent. If the artist who painted the portrait of "Mrs. S. O." for the Academy of 1861, would be good enough to let me see my Lucinda on canvas I might be contented—but not otherwise.

I am dallying with this scene, you see, and trying to conjure up a picture of these two ladies in your mind, because my poor pen feels its inadequacy to describe this first meeting between those who bear such important parts in the history herein written.

I suppose they had heard each other described before—for each recognized the other at a glance.

"This, then," thought Lucinda, "is the doll whom Aubyn is to marry; he cannot, does not love her. And for this child—this pigmy—I am preserving him, and his heritage, at the price of Heaven knows what loss and disgrace to my father."

"So here is Pentowan's daughter," was Emma's thought. "I hate her! She is as wicked and designing as her father—and is in league with him without doubt. But I think I am a match for her."

All this passed in a very brief space—while these rival beauties sailed by each other.

The next morning St. Tude's bell tolled solemnly amid the rain, as the funeral procession wound slowly down from Tresellan, across the bridge, through the town, and defiled in the small and crowded graveyard situated, as was usual in those days of sanitary darkness, in the very heart of the streets, with the windows of sleeping apartments opening on its enclosure, and the upper stories of some of the houses actually overhanging it.

By a strange chance Emma and Lucinda stood side by side at the open grave. And so Sir Abel was lowered to his résting-place.

CHAPTER XI.

FATHER SERAPHICUS.

THE modest cottage of Father Seraphicus stood at the foot of a plantation of firs that climbed the hill overhanging Terini. On either side the trellised vines made a fragrant coolness, where the idle folk of the village took their ease on festal days, eating slices of melon dipped in sweet wine. But at other times the padre's house was tolerably deserted, for the lazy populace dwelt round the little sweep of water they called the Bay of Terini, living on the fish they slothfully trailed ashore in their nets, or on the fruit that grew beside their doors. The Castle of Indolence might have stood in the midst of the hamlet, and would not have been discovered by the inhabitants for a long time, so very sleepy were they. And yet they had the text of labour perpetually buzzed in their ears by myriads of the busy bees Doctor Watts speaks so highly of. There was scarce a hut in the place that had not its little row of hives, whose diligent occupants rifled all the flowers of the rich pasturage, where the cows, as drowsy as their owners, chewed the cud quietly under the shade of alders. Truly, a spot flowing with milk and honey, and where, if anywhere on this earth, the lotos must have lingered among the fruits to drown the Terinites in listless langour.

But though this was the habitual character of the place when it was first seen by Christopher and Gregory—of whose meeting I have little to tell you except that the lawyer mentally wished the clerk at the bottom of the blue Mediterranean; but, as I have said before, he so thoroughly believed in Gregory's honesty (a quality synonymous with folly to his mind) that he would not have scrupled to commit a murder before his very eyes, trusting to be able to persuade him that it was only an action-at-law afterwards,—as these two, mounted on mules, came in a cloud of dust down the steep, winding, narrow road into Terini, they heard much tinkling of guitars, banging of tambourines, and sound of singing and laughter. It was the festa of the patron saint of Terini, and the people were enjoying themselves. It was a lucky day for their arrival. The inn was deserted, save by the sleepy lad who turned their mules into the shed which did duty for a stable. There was nothing to be had to eat—but one need not starve where there are melons and grapes in plenty. As the pair were making an Adam and Eve repast in the garden, Father Seraphicus, who had been visiting a sick person close by, saw them, and perceiving they were strangers, guessed the plight they would be in on such a day. As Christopher had just plucked his second melon, the sound of a gate closing made him turn, and he saw a figure coming through the garden towards him.

The padre was dressed in the long black cassock of a parish priest, his head shaded by a broad-leaved hat, not quite so clerical in character. He was a short, spare man, with a face much lined and furrowed by time or trouble, mayhap both. His eye was still bright, though a deep mark across the upper part of his nose betrayed the frequent use of artificial appliances in the shape of spectacles. A few thin but long locks of perfectly white hair escaped from under his hat, and lay silvery on his shoulder. His mouth had a sweet smile on it, and his appearance was very prepossessing when he approached the fruit-gatherers.

"Travellers, signori?" he asked, in Italian.

"We have come to Terini for a day or so, padre," was the reply, in not over-brilliant Tuscan. "We are intending to travel by the coast to Genoa."

"You are English, I think?"

Christopher bowed an assent.

"I knew an Englishman very well, of the name of Tresellan. Do you know such a one?"

"I did," said Christopher, "but he is dead. I live not far from the family seat."

"Strange," murmured the priest; "I have always asked of every Englishman I have met with. You are the first who has told me he knew him. And you"—the good father made use of one of those expressive Italian gestures, which told quite clearly as words—"and you tell me he is dead."

There was a silence for some minutes.

The priest, his head bent on his breast, was lost in thought. Then his eye gradually stole up from the grass to take a summary of Pentowan. He appeared satisfied with the scrutiny, as who would not? Not one in a thousand would have suspected treachery in that plump, rosy face.

"Was he married?" he asked in a voice so studiously careless that it belied itself.

"He brought a countrywoman of yours to England as his wife—but the marriage has often been doubted. It will cause some difficulty now, perhaps, for there are two sons, one by this Italian and another by a later marriage."

"She is dead, then!" and a sigh broke from the old man's lips, so heavy and so sad that Christopher could not but notice it.

"You knew her then, or why do you sigh thus?" he asked.

The priest shook his head. "Years ago—years ago, as a child."

"Was it a marriage?"

Another gesture, which implied that Heaven above knew; the good man would not commit himself to any stronger assertion.

Just at this moment Gregory came up. When he first heard the voices, he was further up the garden, but hastened back immediately. Unluckily a fine scorpion had selected a warm spot just in his backward path for its siesta, and the creature's appearance, as his hasty step aroused it, alarmed the clerk, who had never seen such a monster before. He jumped on one side with nervous agility, and lighted on what, apparently, was solid ground, but was merely the luxuriant growth of the country matted together at the bottom of a hedge overhanging the road that ran some ten feet below the level of the garden.

So with a crash and a stifled cry for help, our Adam was exiled from the garden rather abruptly.

He rolled into the road carrying a small cart-load of earth, and stones, and rubbish with him, including a few lizards and some smaller specimens of the original cause of his terror, that, sticking up their menacing tails, shambled off among the grass.

The fall, or rather the roll, did him no greater harm than the surprise and the dust it entailed, so, after a shake, Williams picked himself up, and walked off toward the gate to re-enter the garden. When Christopher saw him coming, he hinted to the priest that it would be best not to speak of the Tresellans before him—"for reasons;" and so the subject was turned. Father Seraphicus then made the proposal he had originally intended on approaching them—namely, that they should take up their quarters at his house during their stay.

The devil appeared to be very well disposed to Christopher, for this was the very thing he wanted.

Half an hour after, they were comfortably seated in the priest's modest little study, eating goat's-milk cheese, and drinking a little choice wine that the old gentleman kept in store for the visits of his bishop.

When Gregory was out of the way, Christopher determined to bring back the conversation to its former theme. But Gregory was not to be very easily got rid of; he had heard his host called "Padre Serafico," and he knew that his mission had begun, though he did not quite know what it was, or how it was to be performed.

Christopher's idea was to work on the old priest's feelings, and tell him of the result that the difficulty of proving the marriage would bring about—how his niece's child would be disinherited—and so try to extort the proofs from him before Frank's arrival. You may ask, what would be the use of this if (as would happen on his arrival) further proofs were placed in Frank's hands?—nay, there would be something suspicious even to Frank in Pentowan's presence there under such circumstances.

But Christopher somehow had got it into his head that the old priest would never see Frank. Then his plan would be faultless, for he would be sole possessor of the secret, and would be able to hold the proof over Denzil's head;—at least when he had recovered the forged bill, and he was determined to do that by some means or other.

For several days our rogue was busily engaged in getting into the good old man's favour. Among other methods, he adopted the notion of becoming a likely convert to Romanism, and spent much time with the father in theological discussion.

But he seemed as far from his end as ever. Seraphicus, troubled in mind though he was, to think of the injustice likely to befall his niece's child, was too much on his guard to betray the secret. Nor could Christopher urge it except in a very roundabout way, for was he not supposed to be utterly ignorant of the fact of the marriage and of the padre's share in it?

It was curious that within two days after Christopher's arrival, the father's health began to fail, and he grew mysteriously ill. Had Martha been more careful and not quite so old, her eyes could not have failed to discover when she washed the padre's glass, after he and the lawyer had been discussing a bottle of Lachryma Christi, that there was a peculiur sediment at the bottom of it.

It was curious that two of the ducks that had paddled in the gutter where the rinsings were thrown, had been found dead, and the beggar Jacopo, who made them into a pie, was very ill after eating it. But old Martha only threw up her eyes, and said the birds were bewitched, and laid the blame on that wicked old Annina at San Girone.

It was odd that when Christopher was so forgetful as to leave his purse on the dressing-table, he should have remembered to bring two of the stoppered bottles out of the cabinet between the windows. To be sure, they might have been medicines against sea-sickness, or in case of illness in travelling. At all events, he did take a dose of a night from the bottle containing the thick brown liquid.

At last the priest became so ill, that Martha, still anathematizing that wicked old Annina, felt it necessary to call in old Bajoso, the doctor, who, be it recorded, attended to animals as well as humans, and very often seemed to forget that he was attending to the latter, so violent were his remedies.

He, of course, came in full fig to visit the parish priest, and did not fail to inform everybody of his mission. It was sad news for the poor people of Terini that their good pastor was ill, and, if they had not been so ignorant, it would have been worse news to hear that Bajoso was to attend him.

The symptoms our learned apothecary declared to be very new to him, and not to be found in Galen, though for that matter they might have been for all he knew—his acquaintance never having been pursued farther than the title-page and the back label.

Now, whenever Bajoso met with a disease about which he was ignorant, he had recourse to phlebotomy. Need I say that he bled nearly every patient he came across. But this treatment did not appear to benefit the priest, who, on the contrary, sank and sank, as might be expected of a man of his age.

Most assiduous was the kind Christopher in his attentions to the sick man. He smoothed his pillow and administered his draughts; for Bajoso sent up some feeble cooling potations about as medicinal as ginger beer.

How grateful old Martha was that Heaven had sent the good "Inglese" at such a time! and then that he should have been converted from an "heretico" by her master! "An act of that sort was a good item in one's accounts with heaven, and just before death too"—for it was no longer to be concealed that Father Seraphicus was about to quit all further earthly guardianship of his little flock at Terini.

CHAPTER XII.

"POPPY DEATH."

As Padre Serafico's end was approaching, within a week after Christopher's arrival, the old man grew restless; the knowledge that the secret of his nephew's legitimacy would die with him evidently preyed on his mind. Yet he feared to trust a comparative stranger, and could scarcely believe that Abel had died without bequeathing to some one the means of establishing the marriage to his son.

Late one night, when he was sinking away fast, with no power of moving, and scarce any of speaking, he called Christopher to him, and begging Gregory to leave the room—which he did much against his will, and only because he would not distress the dying man by his refusal—made the lawyer sit beside him on the bed.

There was a grim smile on Christopher's mouth as he obeyed, but the lamp was behind him, so that his face was hidden from the dim eyes of the priest.

"My son," said the old man, "I have but a few hours to live; I have bid Martha send for a confessor to San Girone. Before he comes, let me tell you a portion of what he must hear. Abel Tresellan married my niece—was married to her by me!"

Christopher affected a start of surprise.

"On the night of the marriage, we three vowed on the altar never to reveal the secret, except when it became necessary for my niece's honour to divulge it. The signal that this was the case was to be the ring of Sir Abel. To whomsoever he delivered that ring, to him I was to deliver the proof of the marriage."

("Why did not Denzil tell me about the ring?" thought Pentowan. "Had he done so, he would have saved us all a world of trouble. Nothing easier than to have stolen it from Rewth—nay, we might have got one like it.")

"The ring has never come to me. When I saw you, and heard of Abel's death, I thought at first you were the messenger."

Christopher shook his head.

"No, I know you are not; but I feel I must leave this secret behind me—especially as you tell me my darling's child is threatened with disgrace and loss. After long thought and prayer, I have taken counsel of my heart, and will intrust it to you. Fetch me that crucifix from the window, friend."

The old man lay back in the bed, quite still, with his eyes closed, for the long conversation had wearied him.

Christopher stept to the window on tiptoe, as one does instinctively in the room where Death's presence is felt to be so near at hand.

The moon, coming in at the window, glanced white on the silver crucifix suspended in the recess. It was a very calm night. Christopher could not help noticing it, and paused for a moment to gaze out. The ebbing tide was creeping back with a low whisper among the shingle on the shore. Below in the village but few lights were to be seen. In the offing, a felucca, with her swallow's-wing sails, was gently swaying, as if at anchor, for there was no breeze to do more than just lift her streamer and let it fall idle again at intervals.

Down the path of silver that the moon's reflection formed between the horizon and the beach, a little boat was shooting along, urged forward by the oars, whose dull roll in the rowlocks came faintly on the ear—so very still was everything without.

Christopher detached the crucifix, and carried it to the priest.

"Lift me up, my son."

Very gently, and with slow movements, Christopher raised him and propped him up with pillows; but careful as he had been, the invalid was seized with a fit of coughing.

The lawyer ran to the table, and fetched some of Bajoso's innocuous draught, which he put to the old man's lips. After a minute or so, the cough ceased, and the padre spoke again.

"You must swear to me on this crucifix that you will be secret, and perform this trust."

There was a moment's silence. The ripple of the tide came in at the window, and a grating on the beach announced very faintly that the little boat had reached the land.

"By that holy church into whose bosom I have recalled you, and by the remembrance of the pardon you have received for your heresy, you must undertake this mission for the peace of my soul."

There was a sound of hasty footsteps in the streets of the village, and a sound of knocking and shouting at the inn. But Christopher and the priest were too deeply interested in the immediate object of their interview to observe this.

"I swear," said Christopher, "and bind myself by my obedience to Mother Church and the Catholic faith to do whatsoever you require." And he kissed the silver crucifix.

"Hola, signor, this way, this way!" rang through the open window, and the reflection of a torch passed rapidly across the ceiling.

But neither the lawyer nor the priest noticed it, nor did they heed the hurried steps stumbling among the loose stones that covered the road beneath.

"Bring me that oaken box that stands beneath the table in the oratory, my son."

Christopher stept into the little closet adjoining the bed-room, which was fitted up as an oratory, and found the chest. As he was bringing it back by the open window, what made him pause and tremble, and nearly let fall the box?

It was the voice that exclaimed, "Bring back the torch, quick; curse these roads, I have dropped my walking rod."

Christopher strode to the bed, placed the chest on it, and saying, "Stay, 'tis time for you to take your medicine," went up to the table.

As he poured it into the glass his hand shook, and the bottle clinked and tingled against the rim of the Venetian goblet. When he turned back he was thrusting an empty stoppered bottle into his bosom.

A faint odour of poppies, perhaps from the cornfield on the other side of the road, filled the room for a moment.

"Drink it," said Christopher, quickly; "drink it all."

The old man obeyed him, attributing to the excitement naturally consequent on the oath, and the trust Christopher had just undertaken, the almost rudeness of the command, rather than entreaty, with which he offered the medicine.

"It is strong," said the priest, after he had taken the draught; "it makes my head swim."

"'Twill do you good. But where are the keys? Here, are these the ones?"

"No, there," said the other, stretching his hand toward his cassock, but letting it drop heavily on the bed; "I feel strangely weak and heavy. Hark! what is that?"

"Ten thousand fiends!" exclaimed Christopher, as a loud knocking at the door was followed by the sound of Frank's voice.

If Christopher had been behind Gregory, as he ran down the stairs to the door, I think he would have given him a push that would have gone far to break his neck.

Between you and me, Gregory had been standing with his ear at the bed-room keyhole; and if Pentowan had been on the alert, he might have heard him groaning, as, one by one, the clerk heard his master's lies and pretences revealed. So it needed but three or four strides to take him to the door, through which he soon admitted Frank.

Frank had frittered away his time, goodness, or perhaps badness, only knows where and how. It is enough that, a week behind his time, he was put ashore by a felucca bound for Sicily with oranges and oil, on this very night, to find on his arrival at Terini that the good priest he had travelled so far to see was not expected to outlast the night. Obtaining a guide at the inn, he made his way at once to the padre's, and was, you may easily suppose, somewhat puzzled to have the door opened to him by old Gregory. whose face he had many a night seen through the wreaths of smoke in the "Ship" parlour.

Frank had been in a pretty continuous state of vinous excitement for some time past, so he wiped his flushed face and murmured, "Confound the drink, it must be a trick of delusion." For he positively fancied that his seeing Gregory was a sign of an attack of *delirium tremens.* His wonder was not much decreased when he found Christopher in the priest's chamber.

But our wily lawyer soon explained to the foolish lad, in a most satisfactory manner, that he was travelling to find a market for the cured pilchards he had at Polvadnick—the proceeds of the last summer's seining—when he met with the padre; adding, that when he found he was attacked, he stayed to nurse him out of gratitude for his hospitable kindness.

During this brief but satisfactory explanation, I must confess that Christopher, in kindness to his dying friend, who was lying quite still with his eyes closed, tried to hustle Frank out of the room.

But Frank, who as I said had been drinking, was not to be so easily got rid of.

With an unsteady step, he approached the priest, and, taking a ring from his finger, put it into the lax white hand that lay listlessly on the coverlid.

It was as if the ring were a talisman. The dying man, who had not been able to move, sprang up without an effort in the bed, looked eagerly on the ring, hurriedly thrust the keys into the lock of the oaken chest, turned it, threw back the lid, and taking out a small packet, thrust it into Frank's hand.

"You come from Abel Tresellan's son—this is his ring—the packet—the packet"—— Here his false strength deserted him, and he fell back on the pillow.

"You will find it all here," he gasped. "Say I kept—my promise—I—have—preserved—the—proofs."

A heavy drowsiness seemed to come over him—a lethargy, from which, you could read in his eyes, his spirit would fain have shaken itself free, but the physical power was wanting to aid the mental effort—and he dropped away into a sleep. But just as Frank, on whose arm his head had fallen, was about to lay it on the pillow, the eyes opened—and the priest, grasping the lad's arm with one hand, pointed with the other to Christopher's burly figure standing between the lamp and him, and groaned, "Beware!" And then his jaw fell, his eyes closed, and the old man was gone.

In vain did Martha, the cook, wring her hands and wail. Her master was past hearing even her shrill voice that had so often invaded his study and broken in on his devotions.

In vain did Doctor Bajoso cluck over his late patient, like a hen in a coop, and feel where the pulse was *not* beating—the priest was beyond the reach of either cookery or quackery.

Loud was the lamenting in Terini, and long was it ere the good people forgot to plant the old priest's grave with flowers and wreathe the cross at its head with immortelles.

I think you will remember that I told you Gregory was the son of a small druggist, and was pretty well acquainted with some of the nastinesses he had dealt out as a boy across his father's counter. It was not, perhaps, very safe to let such a lad deal with such dangerous things as some of the articles in demand were. But in those days there were no acts of Parliament to restrict the sale of poisonous compounds—or if there were (for I am not jurisprudent) they were never put in force. So that when busy mothers came for a little "opie" to put their noisy brats to sleep, if the lad behind the counter doubled the dose and made the children sleep so quietly that their parents were never disturbed by them again, nothing was ever heard of the matter.

However, that has nothing to do with the reason which led me to remind you of Gregory's father's trade. I wished to remind you of it, as an excuse for Gregory's apparent impertinence. No doubt, as having once served in a druggist's shop (and I've seen men set up as medical practitioners on no better grounds), he imagined himself one of the profession, and quite on a brotherly footing with Bajoso. If not, why did he take that worthy aside and inquire into his treatment of the late padre? It was, no doubt, the recollection of that old occupation that made him sniff the night before at all the medicine-bottles, and linger so long over the Venetian glass from which the old man drank the last dose he was fated to swallow.

I wonder what the secret of making Venetian glass was? You know, of course, that it had the reputation of breaking when poison was poured into it?

But I'm rambling again. Let me see. Oh! I was saying that Gregory cross-examined Bajoso. So he did, in this wise.

"Ah!" he said, "you gave him so-and-so, and so-and so? Good. Excellent. Only that?"

"Only that, signor. Could your excellency have suggested"—you see Bajoso took the stranger for a medico, and was very reverential.

"Oh, no! oh, no! the best treatment. But you did not add anything else to the draught?"

"Oh, no! signor. Only those."

"You did not put any——" and here Gregory whispered in the doctor's ears.

"None; none, on my honour, signor!"

"Oh!" said Gregory.

Now "oh!" very often says a good deal.

CHAPTER XIII.

"MINE EASE AT MINE INN."

It was but an act of decency to stop and see the padre buried. Christopher hinted thus much to Frank, and was rather astonished, even in spite of his knowledge of Frank's dilatoriness, to find how readily he concurred in the delay. Had the lawyer seen the youth seeing what he saw that morning, he might not have wondered.

As Frank was returning from a bathe, which he enjoyed with great gusto in the gray morning that succeeded the night of the old priest's death, he saw, just as the slanting rays of the sun smote the diamond lattices of the waking cottages to gold, an exquisitely moulded arm draw back the curtain of a window just above him; and a brief vision of a beautiful face and two lustrous black eyes haunted him sufficiently to lead his steps back in the same direction again during the day.

Our budding cornet was susceptible, but a stronger head than his might have been turned by Julia's beauty, though she was but the daughter of a well-to-do oil-merchant. I fancy she must have read love's telegraph tolerably clearly in Frank's face in the morning, for she spent the greater part of the day in gazing out of the window and loitering about the garden. At last her watching was rewarded, and the young Englishman passed. Eyes! eyes! how they spoke a very intelligible language, better than the tongues did when they began to run. For, ere long, the two young people had struck up an acquaintance on I know not what grounds; and the acquaintance soon ripened into something warmer and better even than friendship.

I'm afraid Frank's intentions were not the best in the world when he first laid siege to this young Italian's heart; but there was something in her manner that soon killed the ill weeds growing among the love-in-idleness, and by the end of the week, his affection was honest at least, if purposeless. So when his departure came near, there was a tender meeting to take farewell, that began with all sorts of mutual vows and entreaties. Each was begged to forget the other, and each in turn declared that never-ending recollection was the only possible course to be adopted.

When they did separate—for I cannot attempt to chronicle the scene, nor will I refer my readers to their own experiences under similar circumstances, for no two people ever make love alike. Well, then, when they did separate, Julia had given one of her long jetty locks to lie upon that foolish fickle heart of Frank's, and he, in his turn, had suffered a snipping that would have made his Truefit shudder, as he observed at the next sitting, "'Ad your 'air very badly cut last time, sir."

The time for Frank's departure came when the bell of the little chapel at Terini was swaying slowly to and fro, its melancholy notes falling heavily on the warm hearts of the little flock, to whom it told that their loved pastor was consigned to his last home. A fitful wind was coming in gusts from the pine forest above the village, and sighing over the tiny graveyard. Two tall white lilies were already planted on the pastor's grave, and waved solemnly to the breeze that set all the grasses and flowers nodding.

It was a week from the day on which Father Seraphicus had fallen asleep in Frank's arms. It had been agreed that Frank, Christopher, and Gregory were to travel homeward together. They set out late in the day, later than was safe, several of the villagers told them. Indeed, they had arranged to start earlier, and baggage was packed and horses were saddled, but somehow Frank was missing; and, as he had not chosen to confide his amour to either lawyer or clerk, they could neither of them find him.

Their shadows were long before their feet as they walked up the steep road out of Terini, leading their horses, accompanied by some of the villagers, and followed by the blessings of all the rest, to whom Martha had told frequent and long tales of the kindness of the strangers, and the generosity of the stout one particularly—for Christopher had been very lavish of gold to the old housekeeper—no ill plan of his, so far as gaining her good will and keeping her in a state of mind not prone to suspicion, were concerned. But the good lady would talk; and it was not always well in those days to be spoken of in Italy as a wealthy traveller.

"Press on, signori," said the old sacristan, as he bade them adieu at the crest of the hill. "Press on to Mentazza, where you will find a good inn. But you must hurry, and be careful not to lose the road." So, adding a few instructions as to the shortest route, he waved an adieu, and was speedily half way down the slope of vineyards.

There was, to the right of the road, the pine-forest. Through the gloom of that, a lithe lad, whom the travellers might often have seen loitering about Terini, was running as fast as his legs could well carry him among the crowded slender stems, and through the grass and accumulation of dead leaves on the ground.

Twice on his path a tall figure in a cloak started up, a few whispered hurried words followed, and the lad ran on, while the cloaked individual slouched off in a slanting direction toward the road to Mentazza.

Each of the three riders had plenty to think of, so they kept silence.

Christopher, having laboured in vain over the net he had spread for Father Seraphicus, was busy conceiving new toils for his companion.

Gregory was utterly lost in meditating what he was to do, and how he was to do it, to aid Aubyn to his rights. Once or twice he most dismally regretted that he had ever allowed his good nature to say "yes" to the proposal of this undertaking. At the time it had seemed easier to assent than to deny. Now he felt how much better it would have been to bear any punishment for the refusal than to undertake what he had no possible hope or means of accomplishing.

Frank was drowned in a reverie of the sweetness of love—of which, to tell the truth, he was now really tasting some of the pure sweetness.

So no wonder that, though they still cantered on at a good pace for the wretched Italian nags they bestrode, they discovered, just as the brief twilight was about to begin, that they had all forgotten the directions, and were, in a word, lost. This conviction dawned on them as they arrived at an open glade from which four roads branched off. Each looked at the other for information; but the only information so obtained was that none of them knew the right route.

But luckily a guide was at hand. A peasant, wrapped in a long cloak, was sitting swinging his legs on a rail by the roadside. To him they applied; whereupon, taking the oaten pipe—on which he had been indulging in a discordant screed of music—from his lips, he indicated one of the roads with a grunt, and, vaulting over the bar, walked into the wood.

"Mighty civil!" said Frank, and he began to hum an old air—

"Tell me, shepherd, tell me."

"A shepherd with no flock," said Gregory.

"Perhaps he has gone to them; they may be at pasture beyond the wood."

So they pushed on, along the road indicated.

"It seems to me further than the old sacristan said," grumbled Frank, banging the flanks of his sorry steed with the sheath of his sword.

As for poor Gregory, not being much of a horseman, and accustomed only to a pony when he went about serving writs and the like amenities for his master, he was miserable. Every jolt of the ungainly hackney jarred all the vertebræ in his back, and produced a sensation that I can compare to nothing but the rapid, continuous swallowing of angular crusts, "grating against the nubbles of one's spine."

By and by another peasant in a cloak was found seated most opportunely where there was another divergence of roads; and, thanks to those two guidances, our three travellers arrived by nightfall at an inn, which a lounger at the door informed them was the inn of Mentazza. To be sure, it did not quite answer to the description the sacristan gave, but might there not be two inns in the place? and if there were not, there was no reason why a person who was so clearly in error as regarded the distance might not also be wrong in the description of the place.

At any rate they were tired, and here was an inn.

A dark, surly host ushered them into an apartment of very sombre appearance. A frugal supper of eggs and dried fish, with some fruit, was set before them, and they did justice to it, for it speedily disappeared.

CHAPTER XIV.

MORE THIEVES THAN ONE IN THE WORLD.

SUPPER over, our trio drew round the fireplace, where a few logs were kindled, for the nights were still cold, even in sun-warm Italy.

Christopher called for a flask of wine, which proved to be most excellent. Frank was ready at once to do justice to it; and the lawyer, perceiving a means of accomplishing his purpose agreed to the production of bottle after bottle.

Gregory was fond of his glass, and the good wine warmed his heart; and, as he sat blinking over the logs, half asleep, I think he grew to believe that all was a dream, and to doubt his mission, and his master's roguery.

"Well, Mr. Frank," said Christopher, whose face, despite his caution in drinking, was growing more and more glowing under the influence of the genial liquor, "well, here we are on our first stage homewards. And pray, if it be not a rudeness—which I don't fancy you will think it, considering the delay I have made for the sake of your company—may I ask what this document is that the good father gave you? As a lawyer, possibly, I may be able to give you an opinion—not very valuable, perhaps, but at least legal."

"To tell you the real state of things," said Frank, "I have not yet looked at it."

How could he, when he had spent so much time with Julia?

"Ah! well, we will inspect it by and by, with your leave. Not now, don't rise; pleasure first, business after;" and the lawyer laid his hand on Frank's arm, who was rising to get the paper from the pocket of his overcoat.

"What say you to another flask?" asked the latter, whose natural laziness was nothing loath to be prevented from walking across the room, especially after the long and rough ride of the evening.

Christopher assented; and that flask and another had the required effect on Frank, whose bright eye and flushed cheek told that, in spite of his lately-made vows of sobriety, the old demon was getting into possession again.

Then artfully did the lawyer lead round again to the subject of the document, and Frank rose and walked, somewhat unsteadily, to his coat by the door. As he did so, Pentowan looked at the clerk.

Now Gregory had been quite on the alert when the document was likely to have been produced before, but by this time was growing drowsy. The bright flames licking about the logs grew blurred and indistinct, and he began to nod toward the fire, and wake up staring widely whenever an extra powerful obeisance seemed likely to plunge him into the blaze.

But whenever he so woke, his eyes, by old habit, at once sought his master. The reason of this was that, in office-hours, Gregory, occasionally napping even when his master was present, had acquired a way of sleeping with an ear wide awake. The least stir roused him, and he turned toward his master at once a face full of important thought and attention to the work on which he was supposed to be engaged.

So, when Frank got up and pushed back his chair, the clerk opened his eyes wide, and was immediately master of the situation. But, his eyes having opened while his chin was reposing on his breast, he had the advantage of appearing sound asleep to Christopher, when the latter subjected him to a long scrutiny.

Gregory's mind resembled a slow, shallow

stream, loitering between high banks. Other water-courses babble and prattle, full to their banks, and overflow easily, being generally more observable. But the slow, quiet stream is the one to depend on—it never shows signs of trouble. Thus it was that, without starting or doing anything to betray returned consciousness, Gregory was fully aware, from the lawyer's searching gaze, that the time for action had arrived, and the moment for completing the plot was at last selected.

With an unsteady step, Frank, having taken the sealed packet from the pocket of his riding-coat, returned to the fireside. As he laid the paper on the table, he might have noticed that Christopher's hand was in the action of passing over his glass. It was a strange movement, as though it were an act of benediction, and there was a slight delay above the glass, which tinkled, moreover, as if Christopher's ring had touched the rim.

But of all this, Frank noted nothing, though the pretended sleeper by the fire saw it and trembled. A cold shudder ran through him at the thought that the drowsiness with which he was still struggling might be the result of some such unhallowed blessing.

The packet was suffered to lie on the table where it was placed. For Pentowan made no movement to take it up, and Frank, "with love and wine opprest," was now as careless as Dryden's hero of everything except the present grape-juice and the absent fair.

Christopher was measuring the packet with his eye—gauging its length, and breadth, and thickness, with the intention of replacing it by a counterfeit. But as a sudden thought struck him, his countenance fell. The substituted packet must contain something more than blank paper!

He glanced hurriedly round the room, but no writing materials were to be seen; of paper he had some sheets in his valise in the corner of the room, but pens and ink were needed besides. To call the host and ask for them would be to wake Gregory or Frank—for Frank was now nodding too—or perhaps both. After a rapid consideration of all the courses of action that lay open to him, he was forced to one conclusion. "He must take the packet without replacing it by a counterfeit. But then Frank would be sure to miss it, and search high and low for it. He must, therefore, destroy it!"

No sooner said than done. With a hurried hand he snatched it up, and in another moment it had scattered the red embers at Gregory's feet, and lay smoking and scorching in the heart of the wood fire!

At the same instant a knock came at the door. With an angry gesture Christopher faced the in-comer, who opened as he tapped. It was the host.

"Signori were doubtless tired. Might he show their chambers before he retired to rest?"

Christopher breathed again. As he turned to rouse Frank and Gregory, he cast a stealthy look at the fire. A faint blue lambent flame was just flickering away from the flaky tinder of burnt paper, that tinkled and crackled faintly, as millions of points of fire broke out, quivered and died in the shrivelled leaves.

"It burnt pretty quickly," Christopher internally congratulated himself, as he shook Gregory by the shoulder, at the same time scattering the ashes with his foot, though they had not retained the form of the packet—and—(paper shrinks so when burnt)—seemed hardly half the size it had been.

I verily believe Gregory had fallen asleep in spite of his intended vigilance. He yawned, and stretched his ungainly limbs at all events as if he had been one of the sleepers of Ephesus.

As for Frank there was no rousing him in any way, so they took him by the head and the heels and bore him from the field, whence the other dead men were borne by the host to be replenished in the cellar. But before he did this he showed his guests their apartments. Frank and Christopher he placed in a room at the end of a long corridor, Gregory in a small loft of a place over the stables, in which, from the stamping and snorting, there would seem to have been a great many horses.

As the host passed downstairs again, a rough unkempt head thrust itself out of a closet, and asked, "Have you given the youngster a taste of the vintage of Morpheus, Giacomo?"

"Not I, corpo di Baccho!" answered the other, who did not seem at all alarmed at the apparition.

When Gregory had retired, Christopher set himself to wake Frank. It was no easy task, and an hour was spent at it ere he showed any signs of rousing. Why Christopher, just at bed-time, should have taken all this trouble it is not easy to say, unless the following fact has anything to do with it. The lawyer had taken a stoppered bottle out of his pocket, which had about two drops of a brown oily fluid in it, and had murmured to himself, "Humph! I didn't mean to put it all in. I hope I have not overdosed him!"

Just as Frank began to open his eyes, and recover his consciousness, the lamp, after one or two bright spurts and sputters, went out in the odour of anything but sanctity, and Christopher and he were left in the dark.

There is, be it noted, something in utter darkness that is curiously sharpening to the faculty of hearing. As he sat by Frank's side, Pentowan fancied he heard whispering, or rather the subdued sound of talking under the window. It was perhaps with some vague notion of finding one of the inn servants about, and obtaining a lamp, that he went to the casement. But a few words, which a broken pane gave him the opportunity of hearing, made him pause, and open the lattice carefully. Peering over the ledge, he, with difficulty, for neither moon nor star was there to help him, discerned the host in close confabulation with two or three persons of appearance not likely to cause too great exhilaration in a lone passenger who met them abroad at night. One, with a long cloak and goatskin jacket (for Christopher's eyes gradually grew accustomed to the gloom, and, aided by fear, soon got the range of these suspicious gentry), bore a great resemblance to the gruff shepherd who had in the morning, directed our travellers on their way.

Low as was the tone, and difficult the patois in which they spoke, our worthy rogue soon gathered that the object of their wishes was "the money of the English nobleman." However flattering he might have felt this at any other time, Christopher would gladly now have disavowed any connection with the peerage.

"The younger," he overheard the host say, "is as drunk as Saint Priscilla's hogs, but milord is as lively as a baker's cricket at midnight."

"So?" asked he of the sheepskin, accompanying the monosyllabic inquiry by a wave of his forefinger in the direction of his jugular vein.

The host nodded, and the little knot of conspirators fell a-grinning, making thereby a display of dental organs that would have broken a dentist's heart.

Christopher was cold from head to foot in a twinkling. His first idea was to call Gregory, but he got no further than the door, for it was bolted on the outside. As he gave up the attempt in despair, he heard hasty footsteps departing down the corridor. A sentinel had been placed outside, and was gone to report that the prisoners had discovered their detention. Rushing to Frank, he shouted in his ear, "Up, man; or we shall be murdered!" The shout had the effect of rousing Frank to some extent,—enough to assist the lawyer mechanically to push the heavy bedstead against the door. They had barely done so ere they heard the sound of feet coming along the corridor.

"Where's my sword?" said Frank; and then for the first time they discovered that the host had conveyed their weapons out of the room.

Almost immediately their room-door was tried, but the foot of the bed, wedged against a heavy press, prevented its opening. Then came a loud knocking, and a threatening call to open.

To this the inmates of the room did not reply.

Flinging up the window, they looked about for a means of escape. Frank, now thoroughly awake and completely sobered, managed to crawl along a ledge to the ridge of a low outhouse gable. Christopher, not so sure-footed, followed him with the assistance of one of the heavy damask bed-curtains, hastily torn down, and tied at one end to the window, while the other was held by Frank. From this roof they crept to another, running at right angles to it, and traversing the end of the house. This change of their position brought them in the rear of their assailants, for through a window they could see a knot of about a dozen ruffians engaged in endeavouring to burst open their bed-room door. And then occurred what I am about to tell you in another chapter.

CHAPTER XV.

HIDE AND SEEK.

Enraged at being baffled at the very moment when they calculated on success, the host and his ruffians, after one or two ineffectual attempts to push the door open with their shoulders, had recourse to more violent means. A tall pedestal cupboard of oak at the end of the corridor was pressed into service as a battering-ram, and crash after crash announced its effectiveness. At this crisis, poor Gregory, wakened out of his sleep by the hammering and uproar, leapt out of bed, fumbled his way to a door, which happened not to be the one he came in by, stumbled down some twenty steep stairs, and burst through a sliding partition into the corridor. His sudden appearance created a momentary diversion. As he recovered his feet, his sight still confused by the glare of the two torches which the robbers held aloft, he saw one rush towards him with the uplifted mallet he had been employing on the door. One moment more, and a dull, heavy crash on his forehead filled his eyes with a myriad sparks, of all hues of the rainbow, and his mouth with a strange taste, as if of corroded copper money; the scene before him gave one swirl round, as if it were just engulfed in a whirlpool, and then life and light and the world went out to him. He fell on the floor with a groan, and a little stream of blood trickled out from among his grizzled hair upon the oaken flooring.

When he saw this, Christopher was so horrified that, losing his balance and his hold, he slid down the roof, dropped headlong on another about four feet below it, and, bounding down that like a ball, alighted at last on a heap of straw in the stable-yard. This accident settled one question for our fugitives, viz., how they were to get down from the roof. Frank followed the lawyer's example, in a modified form; and, in a few minutes more, the two were running for their lives toward the pine-forest.

As they paused before crossing the road which lay between them and this welcome shelter, they heard a faint crash and a shout, which announced to them that their room had been forced and their escape discovered. But, once within the wood, they were tolerably safe. Diving into it, they made for its inmost recesses, and at length found a promising hiding-place in the crown of a fallen pine. Here, stretched on their faces, they lay, and had the fearful satisfaction of hearing their pursuers pass and repass a dozen times.

For two hours, at least, the search was prosecuted; but, luckily, the fallen tree was overlooked. At length the sounds died away. Then followed a weary, weary vigil till morn. In the oppressive silence of night, every insect, every stirring leaf, became a sound of torture that grew louder and louder, magnified by the delirium of fear and anxiety. Presently, a few short chirpings told that the birds were waking as the stars went out; and the cold, sharp breath of morning came sweeping through the boughs. Then the purple splashes of cloud overhead got tinged with yellow, grew to white fleeces in a gray sky—and then the sounds of life began, and the moon dwindled to a faint thread.

So, while it was yet dim and dusk, the two rose from their hiding-place, and stretched their stiff limbs.

A ghastly enough couple they looked, to be sure! Christopher's face all wrinkles and creases with terror and watchfulness, and Frank's pale with bloodshot eyes—the result of an intoxication arising from something more potent than simple grape-juice. Making for the opposite side of the wood, our pair hurried on as well as their cramped muscles would permit.

The trunks began to show the sky through; grew fewer and fewer; at last they stood at the verge of the wood.

To leap down into the road was the act of a moment; but what was their astonishment when, from the bank behind them, up leapt their friend in the goatskin, with a shout and a whistle. He had been lying at the edge of the wood, and they had jumped down over him.

They, however, had the advantage of him; for, whereas they were awake, he had only just opened his eyes at the sound of their leaping into the road! So, before he had quite recovered, a good straight blow between the eyes from Frank replaced him somewhat hastily on the spot from which he had risen.

Away went our fugitives again; terribly conscious, however, that there were several in pursuit of them before they had gone far, and still more terribly conscious that they were being gained upon. To be sure, Frank might have gone faster had he been inclined, but he was loath to quit his companion, who was by no means a "swift Camilla" in knee-breeches.

A sound of horses' hoofs approaching in front woke a fresh alarm in their breasts, for they imagined some of the wretches had mounted and ridden to cut them off. Just as they were in the act of again seeking a refuge in the wood, the horsemen came in sight at the next bend of the road. To their delight, they found that the new-comers were in uniform. It was, in fact, a detachment of sbirri conveying a prisoner. At the sight of the fresh arrival, the pursuers halted, and vanished precipitately into the pine-wood.

The officer of the detachment drew up, and inquired into the cause of the fugitive's flight. In as few words as possible, Frank explained. As he described the inn, the soldier laughed.

"The nest this hornet came from, signor, I'll wager. We must return to it as soon as he and you are safely lodged at Ceccina, about five miles hence."

Frank and Christopher were accordingly mounted behind a couple of the sbirri, and the cortége proceeded.

As they reached the crest of a hill, about two miles from the scene of this rencontre, they saw a column of smoke rising beyond the pine-wood. Presently, tongues of flame shot up through the lurid cloud, and showers of sparks rose ever and anon. The robbers had set fire to their den!

It was with almost a sigh that Christopher thought of poor Gregory's charred corpse lying among the blackened ruins; though, it may be, half the regret arose from the conviction that he should never again get as useful a drudge so cheap.

The cocks were still crowing, and the day not yet thoroughly begun, when the little troop clattered into Ceccina. Mine host at the inn of Ceccina was but just out of bed, and his wife had her hair in little screws of paper, as if it had been tobacco, which it did somewhat resemble in colour.

Never, to Frank's thinking, had any fowls such legitimate reasons for cackling over their eggs as the hens of Ceccina; never had pigs died in so artistically-streaked a state of bacon as the hogs of Ceccina; and certainly never was wine clearer, and finer, and cooler than that which he poured down his throat at Ceccina, and which hissed pleasantly as it trickled over his parched and burning palate.

Breakfast over, both Frank and Christopher began to reflect on what had in the last twelve hours occurred to them with all the horrible rapidity of a dream.

All of a sudden, Frank jumped up, went to his riding-coat, felt in the pockets, shook his head, felt again, searched his coat and vest pockets, and finished up the scrutiny by looking into his hat.

At last he broke silence.

"By the horns of Jericho! what's come of the father's packet?"

"Have you not got it?" asked the lawyer.

"Not I, in truth! Let me see, didn't I take it out last night? Did I or didn't I? On my soul, I'm not clear, but I've a notion that there was something said about it."

"True," said Pentowan; "and you would have fetched it, but I stopped you."

"True, for you and we had another bottle, and—and—well, I must have lost it somewhere?"

"You're sure you don't remember anything about it?" asked the lawyer, rather earnestly.

"No more than the dead!" was the answer.

"Nor do I. Yet, stop, now I come to think of it! Yes, I remember! It was lying by your side on the bed, as if it had fallen from your pocket, when I came to rouse you, and tell you of our danger."

"Then it has been burned in that den of iniquity!" exclaimed Frank.

"I'll wager my soul on it!" said Christopher,

with some emphasis, and with a grin to himself aside, for the rogue loved his joke, especially if there were a bit of villany in it.

Poor Frank buried his face in his hands, and his feelings were not, I can tell you, very enviable ones.

Oh! shame, remorse, humiliation, what more bitter lessons are taught than we learn of you, what more cruel penalties paid than you exact of us? As this poor young fellow sat, with his head (still aching from his late excesses) bowed down upon his trembling hands, who of us should be cruel enough to cast the first reproach at him, who of us faultless enough to do so without a twinge of conscience? For my own part, I will not upbraid him, for if the hard things his own heart, wrung by penitence and degradation, is saying to him, are not strong enough to make an impression, I conceive my eloquence is not likely to be more effective. If you have vials of wrath, however, of so effervescent a nature as to decline being corked up, there sits a fit subject for their exhibition in the person of Christopher Pentowan. With the marvellous elasticity of a fat rogue, he has begun already to look plump and hearty after his trials. He sits opposite poor Frank, with a smile on his vulgar mouth, and his head a little on one side, as if he were favourably criticizing a picture. For Christopher was one of those critics of pictures who love to figure before a painting with a candle, throwing the light here and there, with a hand behind it, and tilting their heads to the verge of deserved dislocation. I have seen one of these pompous humbugs, who would invariably go through these antics before two photographs, a pencil sketch, and a chalk head, which he had known for years, and set-to posture-making and light-reflecting as if he had been examining a very gloomy Rembrandt or a dusky Rosa.

So our lawyer sat admiring the picture of misery before him, to which his own hand had added the finishing stroke and main effects.

Presently Frank lifted his haggard face.

"Mr. Pentowan, what on earth am I to do? Oh! that accursed demon of drink!"

"Do you know what was contained in that document?"

"Not a whit more than you do. You remember what the father said—about—about proofs—wasn't it?" Poor Frank's memory was a tablet so often washed with rosy wine that it was not very retentive, you see. Christopher saw it, and took advantage of it.

"Nay, I the rather understood him to say he

had waited for the proof that you were the right messenger."

"Was it so? Do *you* know anything, from his conversations with you, that could lead you to guess the purport of the papers?"

"He was always reserved and silent."

"What on earth am I to do?" asked Frank again, in a despairing tone.

"These papers," said Christopher, in a contemplative way, rather as if thinking aloud than as if addressing his companion, "these papers were to establish Aubyn's legitimacy. But surely that needs no establishing—no question will be raised, no doubt expressed;" then, to Frank, "Look you here, Mr. Frank Rewth, five minutes' more delay in your arrival—but five minutes' failure of the wind that filled your felucca's sail—and you had been too late. A short pause on your way to the father's would have saved you this distress and anxiety."

"That's true," said the other, clutching at this salve for a sore conscience. "What do you advise me to do?"

"Consider the delay to have taken place. The result will be the same. Aubyn will still retain the property, and Denzil will never dream of disputing it."

"'Egad, that's true enough! What you say removes a weight of trouble from my mind."

"I am glad to hear it. But remember, for all we know to the contrary, Denzil may be the rightful heir after all!"

Frank opened his eyes a little at this, and seemed to try and think it over in his mind, but that lymphatic faculty had been too violently employed already, and shrank from the exertion of such a contemplation.

"Well, well, all's for the best! And, after all, five minutes would have made all the difference."

(The reader will have the goodness to credit Frank with the three "alls" in that sentence. As he was speaking, and not writing, he was not so alive to this tautology as he would have been had he known that his words were to be subjected to the searching test of type.)

But Christopher was not inclined to let our dilatory friend off so easily.

"Excuse my telling you as a lawyer, that, as you will have to give some account of the failure of your mission, it would be as well to prepare a brief."

"Oh, dear! oh, dear!" groaned Frank. "This bother will never end! What do you advise me to do?"

"It will perhaps be better," said Pentowan, throwing himself back in his chair, and looking up at the ceiling, as if he were planning his scheme on the model of the crossed and re-crossed beams and boards which formed it; "it will perhaps be better to avoid any mention of our having met at Terini. You can say you fell in with me elsewhere —say here, to decide the matter. Your visit to Terini can be as brief as possible. Say that you arrived the day after the priest's funeral."

"But they will ask if the priest left no letter, no packet with any one."

"You can say that you did not like to press inquiries, especially as the people are jealous of strangers, but that, from all you could learn indirectly, the father had made no such disposition or trust."

"I will do so; but I only hope to Heaven that my criminal folly will bring no evil on the heads of those I love as brothers."

"Nay, set your mind at rest on that score; things will go on as smoothly as if this trip of yours had been the dream of a single night."

"Well, of one thing I am determined: my mission once accomplished, I will ask for the sum of money which my uncle laid aside for my commission, and come back to Italy and hide myself from the world."

Christopher shrugged his shoulders, and set down these words as of no more value than any other of Frank's resolutions—things, like the quaint little figures in certain china cups, which only appear when the liquor is exhausted, to be lost again at the next filling. But there was more earnestness than usual in this resolution of Frank's; for his resolve "to fly from the world" was merely another form of saying that he looked for another world—a world of love—in the lustrous eyes of Julia. However, our lawyer knew nothing of Julia, and dismissed the eremitical vow with the above-mentioned elevation of the shoulders, and so the discussion ended.

You must not, however, suppose that all the events of the last night were not discussed by the pair who had so nearly escaped a terrible fate; but there is no necessity for our going over the old ground again with them.

As for Gregory's death, be sure they spoke of that; but what am I, that I should intrude this poor quill-driver's carrion betwixt the wind and the gentility of a refined circle of readers? No, we will, by your leave, ring the bell for some under-servant to sweep up these unseemly ashes.

The fire has consumed the blood-stained planks of the corridor; so we shall need no pumice-stone, still less a plane, to remove the dark stain.

Before Frank and Pentowan left Ceccina, the sbirri had returned from their excursion to the *pseudo* inn. They had found nothing but smouldering logs, and blackened walls, tumbled and tumbling. They had tracked the hoof-marks of a large body of horse to a shallow stream, to the bed of which the robbers had taken, and marched either up or down the course—which, the sbirri, never over-active, had decided not to make any attempt to determine.

A few days more, and Frank and Christopher embarked on board the good ship "Lizzy of the Lizard," bound for Falmouth. A pleasant voyage to them!

CHAPTER XVI.

AUBYN'S DEPOSITION AND FRANK'S DIFFICULTY.

I AM a pretty good sailor myself, but as some of my readers may not be similarly free from the sufferings of the *maladie de mer*, I will save them the agony of tossing in that very ungainly craft the "Lizzy of the Lizard," which rolled considerably more than "forty-three degrees each way eleven times in each minute," as Sir James Elphinstone said one of her Majesty's vessels did in the Mediterranean. Nay, so tender am I of the well-being of my readers, that I will save them the stuffy, slow journey inside the coach from Falmouth to the Polvadnick cross-road—a journey which, in addition to its other discomforts, was perilous when it lay over the moor—and I think we have had enough, perhaps more than enough, of the gentry who have a profound disregard of the laws of property.

Well, then, Frank has arrived, and is detailing his journey to Aubyn, Denzil, and Emma in the

"Blue Parlour," where the luncheon is spread on the lower half of the table.

When he finished his story by declaring that, as far as he knew, no papers had been left by the old padre, I can tell you the student of expression might have found full employment in watching the faces of the group.

Aubyn's was a look of vexation rather than disappointment, for all he saw in the fact was that his father's wishes could not be accomplished.

Denzil's was a mixture of delight and doubt; delight at the success of his plot, and doubt as to the next step to be taken. As for my miniature Lady Macbeth, she was the least moved externally of all. There was a little more pink in her cheek perhaps, but her eyes were just as blue and impenetrable as ever—two heaven-reflecting pools, lying calm and seeming innocent over what treacherous deeps and what wrecked happiness!

Frank sat with his eyes on the ground, and with cheeks and lips white, for he hated and loathed himself for the lie he had uttered.

There was an awkward silence for some time, unbroken save by the tapping of Nem's dainty little high-heeled shoe on the oak floor, her only outward sign of agitation.

Denzil was the first to speak. He was holding

the extreme point of a silver fruit-knife between his forefinger and thumb flatwise, the handle resting on the table perpendicularly. As he spoke, he slid finger and thumb down it until they reached the table, let the knife fall on its back, and raising the handle until it was once more perpendicular (the point downward this time) he slid finger and thumb down again, and repeated the process *ad infinitum.* It is a simple action, difficult to describe, but I have attempted to describe it because it must have been an important performance, to judge from the earnest attention which not only Denzil, but Emma, Frank, and even Aubyn bestowed on it.

"Of course there remains but one thing," said Denzil, very slowly. "I imagine it is clear to us all what must be done."

"And that?" asked Aubyn.

Denzil did not answer in words, but at once suspending the summersaults of the silver knife, he pushed his seat back, and striding to the top of the table, placed himself in the chair which Sir Abel had been wont to occupy at the head of the table, but which, by tacit agreement, had been allowed to stand vacant since his death.

The act was tolerably significant. When Aubyn first perceived his brother's intention, his impulse was to anticipate him. But in that brief space between thought and its exercise, in that infinitesimal fraction of time occupied by the development of perception into volition, an instinctive sense of the indecency, the folly, of such an act, flashed through his brain, thence from nerve to muscle, and the action was suspended almost ere it began, and all passed in less time than it took me to write the first word of this description.

He looked at Emma. There was nothing to be read in her eyes. They were sealed books to him, for he had never attempted hitherto to read their love, and of all written language the hardest to decipher, and the one needing most perseverance and practice, is that one which is projected outward from the brain upon the lens of the human eye, most especially the eye of a woman. Commend me to a woman's eye for that most baffling secrecy—the secrecy that blinds you by its candour and simplicity. I protest to you, that when Miss Amanda looks up into this writer's face after five—six—I cannot tell how many rapid turns of the room to the notes of the Burlesque Galop; when, I repeat (for the sentence has lost breath somewhat, in consequence of those gyrations), Miss Amanda looks up into this writer's face, and protests that that was the most delightful galop of the evening, I look into the upturned orbs, and read in them an implicit belief that life is all a Burlesque Galop, and that this palpitating cloud of gauze and fluttering ribbon has no wish to change its partner till the final bars. But, then, I see in my "Times'" supplement such tender appeals as "Dearest, I was five minutes too late at the Crescent. Write and tell this breaking heart that you are well and happy." And I know these touching sentences are penned on 'Change, and refer to stock and shares, or are scribbled in thieves' kitchens, and denote burglaries and the robbing of tills. So, when I look into eyes that speak eloquently of a life-long whirling to Weippert's music, I ask myself what speculations in the matrimonial mart are afoot, or what peace-breaking and stealing of hearts are meditated.

(I confess that it does not look well for an author, who protests how little influence "ladies' e'e" have over him, to allow them to lead him away into such a long parenthetical paragraph as the last, and that, too, at a momentous part of his story.)

I was saying that Aubyn, not having taken the trouble to study the language of Emma's eyes when they were open books, could not (nor was it likely that he should) read them when they were purposely impenetrable and untranslatable as the blank orbs of a statue.

Neither could he read much beyond bewilderment in Frank's face, though it had an open expression enough, so far as the mouth was concerned, for the lower jaw had fallen as lax and powerless as if Death himself had loosened the levator muscles.

There was nothing very exhilarating in this survey! He turned to Denzil, who, avoiding his brother's eye, had availed himself of a paper-knife lying on Sir Abel's ink-stand, for the purpose of prosecuting those saltatory experiments to which he had previously subjected the silver knife.

"Denzil! Denzil!"—there were tears in Aubyn's voice as he made the appeal—"Denzil! it is not for the lands and the seigniory, for you shall share them with me; but for the sake of our father, for the memory of my mother"——

"Thank you, indeed," interrupted Denzil, "for the offer of half of that which is mine in its entirety! For, here and henceforth, I claim to be the eldest son, lawfully begotten, of Sir Abel Tresellan of Tresellan. It is for his sake, Aubyn, that I do this painful thing—for his sake, that the consequences of a youthful error be not visited on my father's name, and that the lands of the Tresellans may not fall to those who have no claim to be called Tresellan."

Having accomplished this speech, by which he almost persuaded himself that he was doing a righteous act, Denzil left the room.

What so natural for Aubyn to do as to turn to his affianced wife?

"Oh, Nem!" he exclaimed, "is it to a nameless outcast, spurned of him whom he believed and loved as a brother, that your young life is bound?"

"Would a nameless outcast urge that plight upon the woman he pretended to love—a plight extorted on a false pretence?"

The malicious little fairy, whose own lips had been the first to name her Aubyn's future bride! It is wonderful how a little adversity destroys the memory of not entirely disinterested affection.

"But, good heaven! Nem! you do not believe that this can be so."

"Ask Frank there how idle was the story of this foreign clandestine marriage."

"But my father's—*your* adopted father's dying words, Emma—"

"The pain of his wounds made his mind wander. Or, perchance, an over-tenderness—a foolish, a mistaken thought of atoning for an early fault—made him forget justice and truth, and wrong his lawful son."

"On his deathbed! God forgive you!"

And he turned from her to Frank.

"Frank, you, at least"——

But Frank rushed by him hastily, without a word, snatched his hat, and hurried to the door.

"You, too! Then I am indeed forsaken!" sobbed Aubyn, as he sank into his father's chair, and bowed his head on his hands.

But he had misinterpreted Frank's feelings. He, poor heart-broken sinner, hid his face from the man he had injured, lest he should see the brand of Cain upon his shame-stricken brow. Wild, weak, irresolute, humiliated, the events of the last few moments, so unexpected, so appalling, had tortured him more fiercely than words can describe. But the strongest trait in his character was his weakness; and, near as he was to bursting forth in a penitent confession of his fault, that weakness, and its twin-brother, vanity—self-love—laid a burning seal upon his lips.

With hurried steps he passed across the lawn, down the winding road to the ferry, and flung himself into the boat. As soon as the prow grated on the shingle of the opposite shore, he sprang to land, and ran, rather than walked, to Pentowan's.

The lawyer was seated in his now lonely office. They were no easy glances that he flung towards Gregory's vacant stool, as if he expected to see the gaunt figure seated there. He was pretty sure that the meeting of Sir Abel's real and adopted children, and the history of Frank's mission, would be over by this time, and he expected, he scarce knew what; but, at all events, some complication arising from the unexpected turn affairs would have taken.

It was not exactly surprise, therefore, that was expressed in his face when Frank burst in upon him, with that everlasting query that rose to those weak lips at every change and trial—

"What on earth am I to do, Mr. Pentowan?"

And then followed a hasty description of the interview I have just described. It was no more than Christopher had expected—the only new point in it being Emma's decided repudiation of her engagement to Aubyn. Accustomed to look for motives—and bad ones—in every action, however trivial, Christopher penetrated the meaning of this act at a glance.

Begging Frank to be seated, and, with a wisdom that was the fruit of experience, putting a tumbler of wine (from the stock in the office-cupboard) into his hand, this cunning limb of the law tilted his stool back so as to obtain a good view of his companion's face before he began his speech. It was not Christopher's habit to address a jury that he could not watch the face of. He was wont to stand fronting the jury, sideways to the witness he was examining, at whom he jerked questions contemptuously over his shoulder. As he planted some posing problem in that poor wretch's mind, this oily advocate would take a copious pinch of snuff, and smile blandly on the jurymen, the fingers of his left hand playing an inaudible tattoo on his left knee, conveniently raised for that purpose by the implanting of the sinister foot on the seat, while the sinister elbow reposed on the back, of a chair.

I wonder whether I may relate here an anecdote (not at all *à propos*) of what once happened to Christopher while cross-examining a witness. I will venture it, because any reader who chooses may skip it, and begin at the next paragraph. It was a case in which a horse, borrowed of one farmer, had been over-ridden by another, who had left it at the cottage of a labouring man.

The labourer had done what he could for the animal, but it was in so hopeless a condition that, by order of the borrower, he cut the poor brute's throat. An action was brought to recover the price of the horse, and Christopher was examining the labourer as to his treatment of it. "Had he given it corn?"—"No." "Had he given it hay?"—"No." "Had he given it grass?"—"No." Then, smiling blandly, asked the rotund Christopher, "You gave it the 'coo-de-grass' afterwards?" (that was the way Christopher pronounced French).—"No, I didn't, sir," replied the rustic, in all innocence, "it wor gruel."

And the sublime counsellor became the ridiculous.

To return to Frank and Pentowan. The latter, leaning back from his desk, and thus getting a three-quarter view of his companion's face, spoke thus—

"I am sure, Mr. Rewth, you will give me credit for all interest in your behalf, and you will therefore pardon anything which, coming from one influenced by other feelings, would appear to you intrusive, harsh, or prejudiced!"

Frank nodded.

"We will start, then, from the fact that the paper is lost. It does not matter by whom lost

—indeed, whether lost or destroyed, we may say. The contents of that paper are as unknown to any living being as if it had never been penned. Then it seems to me, having in view this utter ignorance of its contents, and this irremediable destruction of the paper itself, that any person judging himself, no matter how culpably, guilty of its destruction, would be doing an act of no earthly service to anyone, and of incalculable injury to himself, by stating his knowledge. For all the confessions in the world will not assist us to learn its contents, nor will any amount of penitence restore it. Now, on the other hand, a statement that such a paper did exist, coupled with so unsatisfactory (because not circumstantial) an account of its destruction, will give to a certain person or persons, who would otherwise bow, sooner or later, to an inevitable and unalterable state of things, a plausible ground for hopes which we are morally certain can never be realized."

"You mean what's done can't be undone, and least said is soonest mended," said Frank.

"Had those proverbs been legal maxims, I believe I should have availed myself of them."

"But then, poor Aubyn! I can't bear to see

him turned out of his birthright, and by my wicked act."

"Fair and steady! fair and steady, Mr. Rewth. Who told you that it was his birthright; or, if it was, that it was *your* act that deprived him of it?"

"What do you mean?" asked Frank.

"Simply this. Utterly ignorant, as we are, of what the lost packet contained, it is just as fair to surmise that it did *not* prove the marriage as that it did. The papers may not even have referred to the marriage, but may relate to the secret missions with which Sir Abel was entrusted in Italy; and he may, wishing them to be destroyed for his good name's sake, have adopted this justifiable deception in order to make sure that his wishes were performed. Had the real contents been specified, no great anxiety might have been felt to obtain them."

"Mr. Pentowan, you are the most ingenious advocate an uneasy conscience ever retained for its defence."

"Nay, not at all. I only state probabilities. But I can set your mind at rest at once by another hypothesis. From beginning to end remember, knowing nothing of the contents of the lost packet, we are going on hypotheses. Of these none is so probable a one as that which I wish you to listen to now. Granted the marriage took place; granted it was performed by all parties concerned with the purest purposes; granted, too, that the packet contained the evidence of that ceremony in Father Seraphicus's own hand; granted that you negligently mislaid or destroyed it—*yet* your conscience may absolve you from consequences, which I think I can show you are not the consequences of your negligence. The marriage was a secret one, the contracting parties were not of the same religion probably, the priest performed it without the sanction of his spiritual head. Here are reasons enough to believe the marriage invalid. But I will even allow its validity; what, in the next place, is the evidence of its having been performed? I need not explain to you how, one by one, the threads of evidence which supported this fact have snapped or been lost sight of, until all rests on the written testimony of Father Seraphicus. In a word, all depends on the power of a foreigner, an obscure priest, buried in an out-of-the-way district, to draw up a deposition in such a manner as to meet the exactions of the English law of evidence. I stake my professional reputation" (that was a valuable wager!) "that the document was worth precisely this!" and Christopher snapped a snuffy thumb and finger together, highly delighted, as well as somewhat surprised, at the cleverness of his own "devil's advocacy."

"Mind you!" he continued; "all this, of course, depended on the course Mr. Denzil (Sir Denzil I suppose we must call him now) would take. From your description of his conduct this morning, I am inclined to think he had made up his mind to a struggle for the headship of the family. Rest assured, had you brought the document safely, it would only have been to see it torn to shreds by legal fingers, and to watch the absorption of a goodly moiety of the Tresellan rents into legal pockets. You see I can be honest, and say sharp things of my profession!" Nothing that he could say, however, could have injured the profession one quarter as much as two-thirds of all he did was calculated to do.

"Nay, more," he added, after a pause,—for he was so charmed with his own special pleading that he delighted in refining on his arguments,—"by losing the packet you have, in fact, conferred a benefit on all concerned. You have preserved your uncle's memory from the searching inquisition of an adverse counsel, you have prevented an unseemly legal contest between brother and brother. and you have allowed to pass as an act of strict, severe, but yet unquestionable justice, what otherwise would have appeared the result of avarice and sharp legal practice."

But I must close our good lawyer's speech, or he will persuade you and me, as he has already persuaded Frank, that the breach of trust, the sacrifice of honour and honesty which he had made to folly, vice, and cowardice, was one of those good works which bless at once their doer and their object. The result was that our weathercock-minded Frank was whistling "Green Sleeves" with the lightest heart in the world as he left the lawyer's office, and turned homeward down the dark, dirty, narrow High Street of Polvadnick. Ever ready, and pleased, to find excuses to himself for shrinking from action, he found, to his rapture, in the present state of things at Tresellan, a reason for returning, as soon as might be, to the languid skies of Italy, there to dream away a lotus-eating existence lighted by the luminous eyes of Julia.

CHAPTER XVII.

ECARTE AGAIN: A FRESH DEAL.

From dark to light, as regards the skin's complexion—from light to dark, as signifying moral complexion—let us turn from Julia to Emma.

There was in this woman's breast no compunction for the desertion of Aubyn, no sorrow for the anguish she had helped to heap upon him. To look at that *mignonne*, with her baby face and her dancing curls, you would have been inclined to trust your life in her fair little hands. Heaven have mercy on you if you did! It would have been infinitely better to have walked down to the Zoological Gardens (had they existed contemporaneously with our Emma) some Sunday (when your interview would be likely to have fewer interruptions), and then and there to have introduced yourself to the den of the third tiger from the end of the terrace, who, I have reason to believe, is the most hasty-tempered and hungry specimen of the feline tribe to be found on the premises.

It was with the soft, stealthy, gentle step of the striped beauty I have just mentioned, that Emma followed Denzil into the library.

He, on leaving the blue parlour, had at once crossed the hall to seek that bookish seclusion. Emma knew she should find him there; those impenetrable, quick blue eyes of hers had read in his face a craving for solitude and gloom. He looked up, as she entered, from the cushioned easy-chair, into which he had flung himself, crouched together like a wild beast after its leap upon its prey—prepared, resolute, savage!

She came up to him, placed her hands in his, and kissed him on his cold forehead.

Then she hissed out, like a veritable serpent, the hoarse whisper, "Safe! safe! Sir Denzil—my own Denzil!"

"I'm not so sure of that," he growled, making no return for her endearments.

"But I am: certain as death! What would sting most men crushes easy-tempered Aubyn."

And it was true. Never hasty to resent a wrong even from a stranger (however much determined in that case to be righted sooner or later), this blow from a brother's hand had utterly prostrated him.

Of all the tortures that made the castles of the

Rhenish robbers hideous, there could have been none worse than that known as the Kiss of the Maiden. The poor victim was led up to press with his the lips of a fair effigy of the Virgin, smiling so sweetly that he could suspect no ill.

"A touch, a kiss! the charm was snapt,"

and twenty cruel daggers sprung forth to stab and lacerate, while the cruel arms encircling him, pressed him closer and yet closer to that treacherous bosom. The awful paraphernalia of the rack, the thumbscrew, and the iron boot were mercy compared with this.

And so it was that Aubyn felt utterly unmanned at this unexpected cruelty in those on whose love he had felt so sure that he might repose. All of which distress and disappointment the dainty sylph, the witch in fairy guise, had perceived, weighed, measured, and felt assured of.

"Shall I tell you what next to do?" she asked. Denzil nodded his head. "Send a message to him appointing him rooms—say those in the western tower, for instance; with the hint that, after what has occurred, it would be better if you met as seldom as might be."

"What! live under the same roof, and see nothing of each other?"

"I do not intend you to live under the same

roof, Denzil, and that is precisely why I gave you that message. You will see that within twenty-four hours after receiving it Aubyn will have left Tresellan, if not Polvadnick."

"If you think so, it is worth trying."

And a servant was accordingly called, and the message despatched.

"And now what is to be done?" asked Denzil, who, as usual, relied on this decided little woman for his course of action.

"Have you seen Pentowan?"

"No; as matters stand, of course he had nothing to do with it."

"Don't be too sure of that! You had better hear what he has to tell."

So Denzil sallied out to find Christopher. That precious scamp's interview with Frank had not very long concluded; indeed, Denzil had passed Frank at the end of the street, and Pentowan had only just locked away the wine, when his fellow-conspirator knocked at the door.

"I had expected you," said the lawyer.

"I could hardly manage to come before; it would have seemed strange, especially as you and Rewth (the bearer of such good news for me) returned together. Besides, I imagine, from his account of it, you have had little to do."

"There you are mistaken, Mr. Denzil. I was at Terini before Mr. Rewth reached it. I closed the priest's eyes: I received the packet."

"Where is it?" broke in Denzil, eagerly.

"I burned it," said Christopher.

There was nothing else to say, but the lawyer saw he was irrevocably damaging his own case by the admission. But what could he do? The papers could not be produced. There was no other way of accounting for their non-production.

"You burned it! Then may I ask what evidence you have to prove that such a thing ever existed? You will see that Frank's statement, that there was no such charge left in any one's hands, is all I require. You can hardly expect me to surrender that bill on such easy terms."

Christopher did not answer. For some reasons of his own he had not, in a hurried note despatched to Denzil on his arrival, explained that Frank was deceiving him when he said they had not met until at Ceccina. Regard for Frank's place in his cousin's opinion I don't suppose had anything to do with this reticence, but I am quite unable to explain the *suppressio veri*.

Denzil, therefore, gathered that Christopher, arriving at Terini, had found Seraphicus lying smitten with a fever, which, dangerous enough in itself, was trebly dangerous in the fact that it committed the priest to the hands of the doctor. He learned little of the doings of the amateur physician who had tended his last moments and administered his last draughts; but he was told that the packet was given to Christopher when the priest was *in articulo mortis*, and that he had carried it in safety until he fell in with, first, Gregory, and then Frank. Then, perpetually in fear lest they should discover what he carried, or some of the million perils and accidents of foreign travel should reveal the secret, he burned it.

Now, I give Christopher credit for telling this lie with a fair amount of circumstantiality and cunning, to which the mere skeleton I give does not do justice. Denzil was completely deceived by it, although simply for his own ends he feigned disbelief. We shall see what those ends were in a short time.

"Can you tax your memory so far, Mr. Pentowan, as to tell me what the words of our agreement were?"

"I recollect no particular form that was made use of. I can only remember that, in consideration of my services in this very difficult and perilous matter, I was, over and above the payment of my expenses and an honorarium, to recover a certain bill with a questionable signature." And Christopher smiled as he delivered himself of this elegant euphemism for forgery.

"Let me assist you to recal what took place. I think you only need reminding that the documents which each of us wished to possess were to be exchanged against one another; and that we, having satisfied ourselves that no little error had substituted a copy, or other useless papers, for the ones we respectively wanted, were then and there to burn or otherwise totally destroy and make away with them."

Christopher bowed his head; there was no denying it. What a disgracefully retentive memory Denzil had!

So, here were our two friends again playing at the écarté of sin and double-dealing, just as we left them in Chapter VII.

"Listen, Mr. Pentowan! We shall probably agree very well as to our settlement on your Italian trip, with the one exception of the restoration of the forged bill. But, to avoid any trouble about that, we will make it the subject of a small arrangement, which I will explain to you."

Christopher shrugged his shoulders. He was not quite ready to buy the bill twice over; but he listened with patience.

"I need scarcely say that I am about to confide a most important secret to you. Our tongues have pretty potent reasons for not wagging about one another. To be brief, then, my cousin Emma, who was the prime mover and chief cause of my successful attempt to oust Aubyn, has demanded that I should marry her in return for the services she has rendered me."

"A most charming young lady, Mr. Denzil; nothing could be more desirable."

"Thank you," answered the other, curtly; "but there is an obstacle in the way of this union. I am married already!"

All the breath in Christopher's body escaped in a long whistle. Here was a weak point in his opponent's play. But our crafty lawyer concealed his delight by a well-assumed look of bewilderment.

"I don't see my way out of bigamy very clearly, Mr. Denzil."

If Christopher had felt that he damaged his game a little while since, it was Denzil's turn now to feel that he had exposed his hand to his adversary. It was true he still held the forged bill, but Pentowan had two cards to play against it—knave and queen, so to speak, in the shape of the plot against Aubyn and the existence of his wife.

Still, he calculated on the result of the lawyer's playing the first card being too uncertain; for what could be proved beyond an intent to suppress the evidence of Sir Abel's first marriage. So, after all, he fancied the game stood much as it did when he played the bill against the packet.

In truth, he was compelled to take some measures to arrange for his marriage with Emma. Aunt Deborah had been urgently summoned back to Devonshire, and could barely prolong her stay beyond another week.

This Nem had urged upon him this very morning; at the same time reminding him that, the aunt once gone, she could no longer stay at Tresellan, except as his wife. Under these circumstances, she argued, there would be no indecent haste in their marrying so soon after Sir Abel's death—his death being, in fact, the stern and imperious necessity which compelled them to be united.

Without, therefore, entering into any account of his first acquaintance with her, Denzil told the lawyer of his having wedded Martha, who, he allowed him to glean, was not of a very high rank in life, and had no friends or relatives in the world.

"That's so much the better, Mr. Denzil,"

observed Christopher, "for we may come to an arrangement with her, whereas relatives might be troublesome to settle with, besides increasing the expense."

"I may as well tell you that she is foolish enough to be passionately fond of me," said Denzil, with a self-satisfied smirk—poor, deluded, vain creature!—"and therefore no attempt to hush it up with her can be made. She must know nothing about it. She must not only know nothing, but positively suspect nothing, of my intention."

Christopher shrugged his shoulders, and, crossing one leg over the other, nursed his knee contemplatively.

"If we can persuade her to do one thing, I see my way out of the puzzle," he said, after a pause.

"What is it?" asked the other.

"I have a friend who possesses a small coaster—a man not very particular about running as close to the law as his craft does to the wind—a trader on principles that you will find harshly commented on in the books which, in your new capacity of master of Tresellan and justice of the peace, you will have to study somewhat closely."

"A smuggler, eh?"

Christopher nodded, and Denzil scored a trick; but it was not worth taking, and would scarce count to the game.

"If you can persuade her to go on board the lugger, I'll persuade my friend not to let her disembark again until he has put leagues of water between her and Tresellan."

"No violence, though, Pentowan, for the poor thing is doatingly fond of me. As for getting her on board, a word from me will suffice. Why, I can tell her that the lawyers have to come and inspect the property in consequence of my father's death, and that, therefore, she must keep out of the way for a day or so. I can tell her a tried friend will conceal her on board his yacht for me. But what will you do with her? I must know that."

"Why, the truth is, my friend, besides this fly-by-night trading, has a plantation, where he could place your wife——"

"By Heaven! you wouldn't make a slave of her?"

"Not a bit of it! There are plenty of easy berths for a free white woman on a plantation, and that without any degrading employment or hard work," said the lawyer.

Now Christopher's friend, the owner of the

lugger, was the one man in the world whom he loved too dearly to betray—in other words, was himself. The story about the plantation was a fable, but I have no doubt his real intention was to sell the poor woman into slavery, still retaining a clue to her whereabouts, that he might be able to lay his hand on her if he wanted the queen to make the odd trick with.

"Well, then," said Denzil, "that is agreed on, and the sooner it is done the better. When once she is out of the way I will place the forged bill in your hands."

"Agreed!" said Christopher. "You shall see her off by the boat yourself. When will you prepare her for the move?"

But Denzil was either ashamed or afraid to undertake this bit of treachery. You will have observed that, generally speaking, he liked others to do his dirty work for him.

"Well, you see Nem keeps such a sharp eye on me, I haven't been near her lately; and—and I think I'll write her a note to explain matters, and you shall take it."

In a moment Christopher had put pen and paper before him, and our intending bigamist wrote a hurried note, explaining his absence on the grounds of business consequent on Sir Abel's death, and begging Martha to place implicit confidence in Pentowan.

"I have left her to believe that Aubyn succeeds Sir Abel, and takes the estates."

"Quite right," said Christopher. "And now where am I to find her?"

Denzil gave him the necessary information, and in ten minutes' time this worthy *advocatus diaboli* was leisurely paddling up the Perl on the head of the incoming tide, looking at the green woods and their wavering reflex, the white clouds and their tremulous doubles on the breast of the placid stream before him, with that high-removed, patronizing look, which he bestowed on Nature as well as Art. Had he been asked, he would probably pronounce the sky "clever," the water and its inverted images "tricky," the woods "judiciously massed." In short, with a jargon picked up Heaven knows where, and applied at random, Heaven knows how, he would have patted Creation on the back, and doled out qualified praise to the Infinite Universe.

CHAPTER XVIII.

PLOTTING AND PITYING.

MARTHA TRESELLAN had spent but a lonely time of it since Sir Abel's death. Denzil had been able to pay only hurried visits, and at long intervals. She had no tastes or pursuits with which to lighten the weary march of time.

She leaned on the ledge of the little window, which gave a glimpse of the Perl through the interlaced boughs. The limes were here trained artificially to form a loophole, affording a view of the river from the cottage, although too small to permit of the cottage being, in its turn, perceived from the river.

The trees were just bursting into bud—bees, still drowsy with their winter's sleep, boomed by the window on their way to the limes. A few precocious song-birds were tuning up their love notes against the feast of Bishop Valentine, and the gulls alternately whistling and croaking, crossed and re-crossed the opening in the trees, as they hovered over the Perl in their pursuit of the shoals of fish that were making their way up with the flood.

All of a sudden the door below was unlocked, a hasty step came up the stair, and the door of the room opened.

There was genuine pleasure in Martha's voice as she said, "Welcome, truant Bud, welcome!" for she was truly wearied of solitude. It is a long time since I read that thrilling romance, but I have a dim impression that Beauty came to have a sneaking affection for The Beast simply because he was the only biped she had to look at and talk to. If familiarity breed contempt, contempt is quite as much akin to love as ever pity is!

But Martha's look of delight died out in an instant when instead of meeting her husband's gaze it fell on the round rubicund face of Christopher. Nor was that same jolly visage unmoved!

"Martha, is it you?"

"Christopher, how came you here?"

You may guess from this knowledge of each other's Christian names that the two had been more than mere acquaintances at some prior period of their lives.

From a pencil memorandum I find written in Aubyn's hand on the back of one of those old letters, to which, as I have before acknowledged, I owe all my information about the Tresellans, it appears that Martha had been the wife of a tradesman in Porthgrehan, who had the misfortune to become a client of Christopher's. She was a handsome woman at that time, and though she necessarily lacked refinement, our lawyer's coarse mind did not perceive it. Vain and imperious, this unhappy woman was foolish enough to lend an ear to Pentowan's unholy suit. She left her husband to be in her turn after a few months deserted by her betrayer. The husband died a debtor in the county jail, and Christopher having made his last guinea out of him by selling his body to a surgeon, forgot him and the wife he had ruined and deserted, just as she brought him a child.

And this deliberate villany was not the error of hot young blood, but the deliberate act of a man who had already begun to be scrupulous in brushing one long curl over his forehead to hide the crescent patch that Time's scythe had mown bare.

They were cruel words, but not more cruel than well merited, that Martha greeted her false lover with.

At first Christopher was stunned, and " struck-in-a-heap," as an expressive phrase has it. But he was pretty well in the habit of coming, at odd times and seasons, on the fruits of his ill-doings, and soon recovered himself.

A few minutes' reflection, during which he pretended to listen with grave sorrow to Martha's reproaches, served to show him that the discovery he had made was to his advantage. The queen in his adversary's hand turned out to belong to him by rights, and made him feel pretty sure of the game.

"It is too late now, Martha," he began, as soon as the woman's tongue had stopped—for women's tongues must stop at some time or other, when they have exhausted a subject some twenty times over. "It is too late now to make excuses for the past. It will be enough if I can atone for some of the wrong I have done you by aiding you now."

"My husband," said Martha, with a stress on the word, "is well enough able to protect me against the whole world!"

"But who is to protect you against him?" asked Pentowan. "Read this;" and he handed her the letter.

"You know him, then, and of our marriage?" she asked, as she glanced hastily over the note.

"All that and more," said Christopher; and so saying he led her to the couch, and there and then revealed to her all that he and Denzil had determined concerning her.

"It cannot be true!" she exclaimed.

"Put it to the test. The vessel you are to go on board is mine. You can, therefore, trust to my doing nothing that shall injure you."

"No! you have never done that!" she broke in bitterly.

"Well, then, if you need further proof of my intentions, know that I have my own ends in view." And he told Martha of the forged bill, and showed her how, once having got possession of and destroyed that, he could in concert with her make any terms he chose with Denzil for both of them.

To give Martha a questionable sort of credit, she entered into the plan from sheer revenge, whereas the sordid wretch who propounded the plot had no soul for anything higher than to satisfy his itching fingers with gold.

At length having determined on their course of action, the former lovers, the present complotters and fellow-intriguers, parted. As Christopher rose to go, a sudden recollection seemed to strike him.

"The child—the girl—what became of her?"

"It was a boy, you affectionate parent and faithful lover, and he is gone—Heaven only knows where! I left him with some people to nurse, and when I tried to find them again some three years since all trace of them had disappeared."

"Poor little devil!" were the only words of regret that this fond father flung after his vanished offspring, as he left the room.

Half an hour after he was at home again. Directly on his arrival he mounted to the garret, from which Lucinda and Gregory had watched his departure in Gibbet Simon's boat. Sweeping the horizon with his telescope he at last discerned a speck far to westward. A little closer scrutiny enabled him to make out that it was a lugger.

"Just at the nick of time, by Jove!" he chuckled, and proceeded immediately to fish an old red sailor's shirt from a corner of the attic. Fixing this to a pole, which he thrust out of the window, and lashed to an empty crate that stood underneath, he gave one more scrutinizing glance at the lugger, and left the garret, locking the door after him, and taking the key. He was not exuberantly delighted on reaching his office to find there Aubyn sitting moodily over the fire, stirring it with a pertinacity that bespoke rather abstraction of mind than any occult impulse anticipatory of a coming race of stokers, whatever Darwin may say about the Development of Species notwithstanding.

As soon as he saw the lawyer, however, Aubyn put down the poker (not without an awkward blush, as he saw how he had raked all the fire out), and began to ask his opinion on what had occurred at Tresellan.

To do him justice he neither understated nor overdrew what had happened. Christopher shook his head as gravely as Lord Burghley—questioned, cross-questioned, put cases, and erected pleas, as if he were interested heart and soul in restoring Tresellan to Aubyn. His endeavours seemed so friendly and so earnest, his astonishment so real and regretful, that he completely deceived the other. It would have been little credit to a life's experience in legal practices had he failed to delude so simple a client.

The result of the interview was, as might have been expected, the extinction in Aubyn's breast of the faintest and most infinitesimal flicker of hope that remained. With a heavy heart and weary step he left the office. The rough fishers and their wives watched him as he paced slowly along the streets, and many were the blessings, none the worse for their uncouth expression, that followed him as he went.

For of course by this time—it was high noon—the whole of Polvadnick was in possession of the change that had taken place at Tresellan. A hermit who lives entirely alone, and has no one to black his boots (if he wear such things), run on errands, clean his plate, make his bed, cook his dinner, or answer his door for him—he, I say, may possibly fall out with himself—even come to blows with himself, and the world not know it. But if he still retain one failing of mortality that requires the ministration of a second person, let him be sure his domestic differences with himself will be as publicly known and discussed within a circle of twenty miles as if they had been proclaimed from the house-top.

Mind you, I am not by this intending to say anything severe of that hard-working body, servants. I think it only fair retaliation that they should discuss us and our doings as we do theirs. What right on earth have we to know whether Jane has a young man or no, if Thomas goes to meeting or to church, if James "walks with" the housemaid next door, and what money she has saved? What right have we to measure the quantity of ribbon Sarah may wear in her cap, or gauge the area of Mary's crinoline? If these things must be looked to, there is a way of doing it, that instead of making it disagreeable to all concerned, constitutes it a bond of sympathy between employer and employed, with esteem on one side, and respect on the other.

I think it is very likely, considering that Emma was the ruling domestic deity at Tresellan, that the servants' hall was only wreaking its just vengeance on the family by talking over the events of the day. Whose the ear was that gathered the conversation that took place in the Blue Parlour, through the medium of the key-hole, I have no means, at this remote period, of ascertaining; but it is quite certain that it was reported as accurately as if it had been a debate in her Majesty's Commons House of Parliament, anent the estimates or the Commercial Treaty, or the road between Bayswater and Kensington Gore.

In declaring one thing the servants' hall was unanimous (and that is more than the said Commons House of Parliament was ever known to be). From Mrs. Tregellas, the housekeeper, to little Joey Varcoe, the stable-help, all protested that it was a thousand shames that so good and kind a gentleman as "Master Aubyn" should be passed over by that odious "Young Denzil." They protested it to one another, they protested it to the various little tradesfolk, who found endless meaningless errands to excuse their coming up to the house. They were a protestant community that it would have delighted Lord Shaftesbury to clap eyes on.

Enthusiasm is contagious. No wonder the tradespeople in their turn lifted up their eyes, and clucked, like so many hens in a barn, over the turn affairs had taken. Trade was flourishing in Polvadnick for the day, as it had never flourished before. Endless were the demands for sand-paper, rushlights, red-herrings, bulls'-eyes, and tobacco, and innumerable the halfpence thus expended by a foolish populace on the luxury of seeing the whites of Mrs. Nancy Barnicutt's upturned eyes, and hearing the crepitation of Betty Vian's usually voluble tongue, or the sonorous grunts of Rozzy Nancarrow's deep bass voice, in the miscellaneous stores, in which respectively these three worthies exemplified the working of the laws of demand and supply.

Hence was it that somewhat to his surprise, and unmistakably to his annoyance, Aubyn found himself the centre of pitying looks, and the object of respectful but commiserating remarks.

He was not at all sorry when the ferry was crossed, and the hall of Tresellan reached. Here at least he hoped for a few hours of undisturbed meditation. But his hope was not to be realized.

Scarcely had he entered the hall when Mrs. Tregellas, with "obsequious sorrow" in her face, came bustling up to him, with a most earnest but humble request that he would give her five minutes' conversation in her room.

"You must go to my brother, Mrs. Tregellas, —he is the head of the house now"—and his voice broke and faltered.

"I come from him, Mr. Aubyn dear," said the good-hearted old dame, her spectacles growing suddenly dim with a mist of sorrow.

Without another word he followed her to her apartment, where with all the tact she possessed the dear old soul endeavoured to give in the least painful way the message which Denzil had sent Aubyn, as you remember, in the morning, at Emma's suggestion, but which Aubyn had left the house too hurriedly to receive.

It was in vain that Mrs. Tregellas put the first part of the message into a fresh form, as "a desire that for Aubyn's comfort the suite of rooms in the west turret should be placed at his entire disposal:" there still remained the undisguisable sentence that "after what had occurred it would be better if Aubyn and his brother met as seldom as might be."

Mrs. Tregellas fairly broke down in her attempt to gild this bitter pill.

"Will you give it to me, my dear madam," said Aubyn, courteous to age even in his distress. "Will you give it to me in Denzil's own words, please?"

She did so. A little flush passed over his face, and died away, leaving it quite pale. He left the room without a word, but returned a quarter of an hour afterwards to tell the tearful old lady that he had packed his few things in a portmanteau, and wished to have them sent to the "Ship" in the course of the evening.

So walking out of the hall door he turned round, gave one last look at the home he could no longer call his own, and then hurrying out through the gate, disappeared in the gathering mists of evening.

CHAPTER XIX.

THE CAPTAIN OF THE "FLYING SPRAY."

When one has an abundant supply of harassing things to think about, time does not hang heavily on hand. There is no greater mistake than to fancy that the days fly fast when we are happy, and lag dreadfully when we are miserable. I am writing this chapter at the open window of the —— Hotel, at ——, and I dare say am set down by the three young ladies in round hats on that seat on the Parade outside as a commercial gent., giving a detailed account of his business tour to his employers in London. Let those three young ladies blush for their error when they see these lines.

Well, as I sit here I see Claude Featherstone, of the Audit Office, taking the sea air with his bride. They have been married five weeks last Wednesday. But I have seen Claude yawn five times in three turns along the esplanade, and I believe firmly that on the three occasions, when Mrs. F. scratched the side of her delightful little nose with her crochet implement, she only did so to conceal a gape.

Now, on the other hand, there is that young De Ffessit of the 171st Foot (the Swampshire Snuff-colours), smoking one of the hotel cigars on the beach below. I know he is staying here chiefly because he can't pay his bill and leave. He is aware that Shears and Broadcloth, of Bond Street, have discovered his whereabouts, and that Moss is unwilling to "fvait for de monish" any longer on that very over-expired bill. What is he saying to himself when he sees Basham? Basham is a member of a legal firm, and always comes down here on Saturday afternoons in company with the "Illustrated News" and "Bell's Life." "By Jove! what, Saturday come again! Gad, how time flies!"

By all of which preamble I am making way for the fact that Aubyn had now found himself two Sundays running sitting in Christopher's pew, and was no nearer a decision as to what he should do with himself than he was the day he left Tresellan.

I have not the slightest belief that it was out of compunction for his ill deeds to him that Christopher had offered Aubyn not only a seat in his pew, but a room at his house "if he would accept it." It was simply and solely to keep him within reach in case Denzil's play (I like to keep up the *écarté* simile) should force him to have recourse to a heavy trump.

Aubyn had first declined the invitation, preferring to chew the cud of bitter fancies in such privacy as the coffee-room of the "Ship" afforded. Nor was that a very contemptible privacy. I don't believe that more than three travellers a month put up at the "Ship," and when they did they generally preferred the inn kitchen with its cheery fire and sandy floor to the damp, smoky coffee-room, adorned by four bright brass spittoons, a smoky chimney, shedding blacks everywhere with lavish generosity, and a picture of the funeral of "Her late gracyous Majestie, Ann." It was a blank, comfortless room enough, and the only thing to be got by occupying it was the information of the decease of her gracious majesty aforesaid; but Aubyn was quite content with it.

But when the second Sunday came and Christopher renewed his invitation, Aubyn for good though not weighty reasons—in fact, the condition of his purse—accepted the offer.

Accordingly, on the Monday his scanty baggage was transferred from the "Ship" to the lawyer's house. The next day was the day fixed for the wedding of Denzil and Emma—for that they were to be married was now no secret. At first Aubyn had been a little pained, shocked would be perhaps a better word; but on deliberation began to make excuses for Emma, who had now only Denzil to look to, Frank having given out his unalterable determination to make Italy his home in future.

There was no jealousy or disappointment in Aubyn's feelings on this question. The jealousy-producing powers of love are like the sleep-producing powers of opium. Without love or laudanum a man goes on well enough, without any disturbance of his natural state of mind. A small dose of the narcotic, and he sleeps like a top; a restricted amount of affection, and he is as green-eyed as a Spaniard. But increase the quantity of the drug or the passion and in the first case the patient becomes painfully awake, and in the second as easy and unsuspicious as the boobies and noddies of a newly-discovered island.

Aubyn was in the position of the gentleman to whom syrup of poppies has not been administered, whether in large or small quantities. Nevertheless, he had no intention of being present at the ceremony; nor although he was rather astounded at Frank's declining to "assist," did he at all meditate setting that youth an example. For Frank had, without a moment's hesitation, expressed his strong disapproval of Emma's conduct, and at once fixed his day of departure for Italy for the day before the marriage.

On this Monday, therefore, as Aubyn was about to knock at the lawyer's, Frank came up to him to bid him good bye.

"May you prosper, Frank," was Aubyn's valediction. "Yet I regret that you should have determined to abjure the profession of arms, my lad—you, so well fitted for a soldier."

"These are times of peace,"* answered the other; "and what need, then, to masquerade in scarlet and lace? When my country really needs my sword, it will be at her service just the same."

"Ay, doubtless," was the reply, "but a gentleman farmer is not certain to be an efficient officer. Your scythe beaten into a sword is but an ungainly weapon after all, and you might have had the pleasure of commanding me perhaps, for I think it not unlikely that I shall end by serving the king's grace as a private in the dragoons."

* The treaty of Aix-la-Chapelle had been concluded about two years.

"Egad, Aubyn, you take my breath away with your easy philosophy. One would not suppose you had just lost your birthright and your bride elect, to see how contentedly you take to life's dark side of the road. Teach me your philosophy, Aubyn."

"An easy conscience, and a belief in Heaven's wisdom."

How a random word flies straight to the joints of one's harness at times. An easy conscience! The expression found out the weak point in Frank's armour, and pierced him like an arrow.

"Aubyn, I want you to promise me something."

"Don't ask me for acres or guineas, and I will promise."

"If ever hereafter you find I have done you a wrong, forgive me. I have so often injured people unintentionally, that I should feel more at ease if I left you with the assurance beforehand that you at least will forgive anything I have done to harm you."

"Granted a thousand times over, dear old Frank. I'm ashamed you should ask a favour that costs me so little—as if it were likely that you had harmed me."

Frank wrung his cousin's hand in silence,

and so they parted. Aubyn watched his retiring figure from the window till he turned down a lane leading to the quay; and that was the last time his eyes ever rested on the man who had done him so great a wrong in return for such a warm affection as does not always fall to the share of a brother indeed.

Scarcely had Frank's figure disappeared when Aubyn's attention was attracted by a sight not often seen in the streets of Polvadnick. It was a detachment of soldiers. Quaint, queer figures they were too, though I do not suppose people in those days thought them so any more than we in our enlightened age consider that there is anything peculiar in a huge, heavy bearskin that is chiefly conducive to unsightliness and vertigo. The way in which the "food for powder" was dressed in those days was perhaps as sensible (if not more so) as the mode in which we serve it up. The men wore gaiters — infinitely more healthy than loose flapping trousers—and the lappels of their coats doubling back all across their chests were excellent protections against the cold, which single-breasted button-up tunics are not, I fancy. As for their sugar-loaf hats, of which the last copies linger on the heads of fifth of November effigies, I will give them up to ridicule; but you will be pleased to remember, that from the day, when Adam first tied a plantain leaf on his head to protect him from brain-fever, to this present writing, mankind has never devised a sensible head covering. After all, the comical conical caps of George II.'s soldiery are certainly not more unreasonable than our black bearskin monstrosities.

The detachment, which marched into Polvadnick, consisted of no more than twenty men, a non-commissioned officer trailing his halberd, and a captain, carrying his half pike. The stir caused by Sir Abel's death, and the successful runnings of several contraband cargoes along the Polvadnick coast, under the very nose of one of His Majesty's cruisers, formed the immediate cause of their being sent to the town. Christopher, I am sorry to confess, was anything but delighted at their appearance, and mentally billeted them on much warmer quarters than the town-hall of Polvadnick, which was converted into a barrack for the nonce by the introduction of some trusses of straw from the stables of the "Ship."

Christopher was the more savage because they had selected that day for their arrival, on which it was absolutely necessary to get Martha on board the lugger which was still cruising about off Polvadnick, but which of course could not now stand in as near shore to take her passenger on board, as Christopher had intended.

To give notice of the arrival of the soldiers to the crew of the lugger was the first thing our friend had to do, and he did it by displaying a black cloth from the garret window.

About an hour afterwards, Christopher, who was sitting at dinner with Aubyn, was called out to see a client in his office.

Generally speaking, our rascal loved his meals and was loath to leave them for the best of clients, but this time he made no demur.

On entering the office he found there a tall woman, apparently a fishwife, for some salmon peal and a mullet were lying in a basket by her side. But no sooner had Christopher bolted the door than the amazon, taking off her bonnet, revealed a brown weather-beaten face frilled by a pair of curly black whiskers that could only have belonged to one of the male sex. It was the captain of "the lugger 'Flying Spray,' bound from any port at which she could get a cargo to any point where she could land it," as he described the good craft, of which Christopher was a part-owner.

"Well! and what are these 'long-shore sharks

poking their noses into Polvadnick for, purser?" The captain always called Pentowan "purser," and seemed to think it rather witty to do so.

"On the look-out for contraband cargoes, Bowser, I imagine, and perhaps for those that run them!"

Bowser laughed, and lifting his gown to an extent that would have been highly indecorous in a respectable fishwoman, he put a foot on either hob of the fireplace, and said, "We'll consider the tank first, purser, and then overhaul the other business." By which this nautical gentleman intended to say that he should prefer a glass of grog before he discussed the matters which were to be considered.

Christopher rose, filled a tumbler of rum and water, and put it on the mantelpiece.

"Those are fine fish," he observed, as his eye fell on the basket; "where did you get them?"

"Why, I wanted something of the sort to complete my character-dress; so I mentioned my requirements to that young limb of the evil one that you must have picked up in some marvellous school for scoundrels, purser. Odds bobs! He brought me these in half an hour's time; stolen, no doubt, from somebody's nets."

"I must cultivate that talent of his."

"You're welcome to the lot here, purser."

The lawyer accepted the gift with pleasure. He was going to carry them into the kitchen at once, when a thought struck him.

"I say, Bowser, I suppose you can't clean a fish?"

"Not I!"

"Because, when one buys of a fishwoman she always does that part of the business; and they'll wonder why you didn't do it."

"Oh, if that's all, the young limb can do that. Just put your head outside the door and whistle so!" and he gave a sample.

Christopher did as he was desired, and in a moment from round the corner of the house darted a ragged urchin, with brown roguish eyes—no other than the lad whom Denzil, as I told you in an early chapter, found disporting himself on the lawn before his wife's cottage.

"Here, Kit," said Bowser, "scrape these;" and he flung him the fish. "By the way, purser, I fancy you must have been the young imp's sponsor; he's called Kit, you see."

"I never knew it before; and I daresay you gave him the name."

So the boy was furnished with a knife, and set to clean the fish on the step of the door leading into the yard. Christopher's office was as full of doors as a rabbit warren is of bolt-holes. It was very necessary, for the people of Polvadnick had a traditional horror of being seen going into a lawyer's office, and would take as many precautions to get in and out unseen, as if they were going into a pawnbroker's for the first time in their lives. This office had four out-and in-lets. One door opened into the house, another into the garden, which had a gate leading out on the cliff; a third, the regular office entrance, afforded egress into the High Street; while a fourth, that at which the boy was posted, admitted into a small yard, which in its turn gave an exit into a small court, through a gate that was generally kept barred on the inside. I suppose the two smuggling worthies did not regard the small boy's presence, for they talked away quite unreservedly although he was just outside the unlatched door.

"Well, purser, what about the woman? I thought you had given up the petticoat ever since that affair with the pretty mercer's wife."

"Oddly enough it's the same woman. But this time I have nothing to do with the matter. The fact is, young Tresellan married her in a weak moment some years ago, and now, as he has come into the property, wants to make a more suitable match; so I have undertaken to get her out of the way for him."

"In return for which——?"

"Well, I want to get hold of some unpleasant papers that are in his hands."

"Oh, I see! Remarkable and fortuitous resemblance of handwriting, eh?"

"Well, something of that sort. Now what I want done with her is to get her off to the plantations."

"Where? I thought you were only going to send her over to Holland!"

"That was my first intention, but I've abandoned it on reflection. You see, she doesn't fancy that I mean to let Tresellan marry. I told her as soon as I had got the bill I would put her on shore again. She's very ambitious, and when she finds out the truth, will play Davy's delight, and will be wanting to be mistress of Tresellan. The result will be a crash, and the downfall of young Denzil, whom I look upon as a comfortable little income for the rest of my natural life."

"So, in order to ensure against her killing the goose with the golden eggs, you are going to send her across the seas! Well and good! I think I can manage that trifle for you. Little Jacques St. Lou will be at Brest about now, and he will do anything to oblige me in the colonies!"

"Many thanks; she shall go on board to-night, so have a boat waiting at the old creek. And, by the way, in case the young Tresellan doesn't keep to his bargain (he's a slippery customer), if I send this ring to you at any time, let her come ashore with the bearer."

"All right, purser. Now, young Kit of knavery, have you done those fish?"

The boy brought them in, took a small coin that the lawyer offered him, bobbed his thanks, and was off at the top of his speed to invest it in "mess," as the natives of Polvadnick were wont to call tarts, gingerbread, sweetmeats, *et hoc genus omne*.

Bowser resumed his bonnet and basket, and left the office, while Christopher returned to eat his dinner and anathematize internally the commandant of Plymouth for sending the soldiers to Polvadnick just when he and Bowser had so much to do, and were so anxious not to be interrupted or interfered with.

CHAPTER XX.

ONE FOOT ON SEA AND ONE ON SHORE.

It was a beautiful night. The moon silvered a pathway fit for fairy feet to "the yellow sands" of St. Erdan's Cove, and the tide stole upon the shore in tiny waves, that broke, scattering sparks of phosphorescent light, with a scarcely audible sigh, at the foot of the Chough Rock, and along the gleaming semicircle of shore to the promontory at the other extreme of the Cove—a steep and inaccessible pile of rocks, called, from some fancied resemblance to a church tower, "St. Erdan's Belfry."

It was to the strip of sand enclosed between these headlands that the boat of the "Flying Spray" was shooting rapidly along with muffled oars. Its course, though not perceptible to the ear, was very clear to the eye. Every blade that dipped the surface caused a flash of "sea-glare" (as the smugglers called it) quite vivid enough to light up the faces of the rowers brightly. Under the bows a liquid fire was churned up, that danced in blue lambent gleams along the side of the boat, and lingered some moments in the broken waters in her wake, as though it were a miniature copy of the Milky Way, that wavered faint and pale across the sky overhead, like a silver ribbon fluttering among the folds of Night's purple robes.

There were three people in the amphitheatre of rocks waiting the arrival of the lugger's boat—Denzil, Martha, and Christopher. The latter was much too thorough-paced a rascal to be open to the influences of nature. The phosphorescence of the sea was far from interesting or pleasing his sense, critic of the beautiful as he pretended to be. On the contrary, as the glittering wake of the boat rolled on the quiet swell of the tide, he was objurgating it strongly in his own mind as a childish freak of Nature, of which the only use he could discover was the entailment of extra risk and difficulty on the already sufficiently hazardous and arduous profession of smuggling.

Denzil, on the other hand, was susceptible of the influence of the hour. His affection for Martha was his strongest passion next to avarice and love of power. He only sacrificed that affection to the still mightier affection he nourished for self.

So the sacrifice was not made without pain, and the pain increased tenfold as the time of parting grew nearer. He hung over Martha, and spoke more tenderly to her than he had often done when he would have been horrified at the thought of deceiving or deserting her. She, too, yielded to the sway of the season and the situation, and for a while dismissed suspicion and revenge from her heart, as only a thoroughly vindictive person can do, with the certainty of not finding the determination at all rusted by disuse.

I shall not trouble you with a detailed account of their loving conversation, for I don't think the love passages of those we like interest us much when chronicled in black and white; and I don't think the distaste, with which all readers of taste must, in conjunction with me, view this precious pair, is at all calculated to endow us with patience to go through a narrative of their endearments. I cannot picture to myself the sort of mind which would find any pleasure in perusing the history of the domestic love of a pair of leopards or hyænas, or take any interest in the mutual tenderness of a couple of pythons.

So, if you please, with a wave of my pen I transport the keel of the "Flying Spray's" quarter-boat to the shining sands of St. Erdan's Cove.

"What cheer, purser?" was Bowser's greeting as he stept ashore.

"None, save a foggy day and a fair wind down channel when you want to sail! Have you no news?"

"Odds bobs, purser, that have I, and news that is likely to delay the fulfilment of your kind wishes for good weather when I start; for I shan't start for three days or so. There are three frigates cruising between the Land's End and Rame, so I must slip into the old lurking-place before morning, and make all snug until the tenth, when that confounded lamp will be taken down to be trimmed." And the smuggler shook his fist at the moon.

You may take my word for it, Christopher was not over-delighted at this news, and entertained feelings towards his gracious majesty's cruisers that were anything but creditable to him as a British subject. Nor was he much better pleased when Denzil expressed his intention of accompanying Martha on board. "It was a lovely night, and he should enjoy being on the water."

Of course the lawyer could not openly oppose this decision, but he did all he could to thwart it, short of that. He had intended, on their walk back to Polvadnick, to ask Denzil for the bill, having a great belief in the efficacy of that timely operation described as "striking while the iron's hot." So all he could do was to take Denzil aside, and say, "I have done my part of the contract; now do yours, and give me the paper."

Denzil laughed. "You don't imagine I trusted myself in the company of smugglers—no offence, I mean the boat's crew—at this time of night, with such a valuable document as that on my person. Call on me at Tresellan to-morrow afternoon, and you shall have it."

So saying he stept into the boat, and seated himself in the stern, by the side of Martha.

"Good night, purser," said Bowser, as he came to where Christopher was standing to bid him good night; and he added in a lower voice, "Any more orders to give?"

"No; though, upon my soul, I have three parts of a mind to ask you to cut that young viper's throat, or ship him off to the plantations with his light-of-love!"

"What wring the neck of the goose with the golden eggs, or transport it to a climate where it couldn't lay! I would not wrong you so much. Won't he deliver up the papers? If you like I'll take them by force when he gets on board the lugger."

"He has not got them about him, confound his craft."

"Well, then, you must wait patiently till you have a better chance. I must not stop longer, or he may suspect. Good bye, purser!"

With that the bluff captain jumped into the boat, which a few sturdy strokes soon carried out of speaking distance from the shore.

Christopher returned in no very good temper. He did not like Denzil's laugh; he began to see that if he did not make haste and score some points, the game was irrevocably lost to him. He fancied he perceived an intention on Denzil's part to retain the bill, and hold it *in terrorem* over him "for the term of his natural life." He had begun to respect his opponent's play; what he had been inclined to attribute to a beginner's luck at the commencement of the game, he was growing to believe premeditated *coups de jeu.* Yes; there was no doubt of it, the younger head was not a whit less shrewd than the elder one; and this once granted, it followed that the former would do all he could to prevent the latter's forcing his best card. The more Christopher thought the matter over, the more convinced he felt that this was the line his adversary would follow; and the conviction did not act as a sedative to his ill temper.

As he reached the top of the cliff overhanging the Chough Rock, he was somewhat startled to find the urchin who had come to the office with Bowser sitting on the edge of the cliff, with his legs dangling over the precipice. To avenge himself for the surprise, and in no way reluctant to vent his angry feelings, Christopher laid his walking-cane smartly across the lad's shoulders as he was scrambling to his feet.

"What are you doing here, you imp of darkness?"

"Don't do that again!" snarled the young savage, jumping out of his reach, and arming himself with a sharp stone.

"What are you doing here?" repeated the lawyer, a little more mildly, for he had a respect for the boy's aim with the ugly missile, after the proofs he had had of his general handiness and acuteness.

"Cap'n Bowser told me to watch if the sojers came," was the surly answer. It was a deliberate falsehood be it known, the real fact being that our young friend was prosecuting his ornithological studies by robbing the choughs' nests, when he saw the meeting on the beach. Curiosity not being a virtue, and he being possessed of a smattering of all the vices, he determined to watch what was going on, guessing at once that the captain and Pentowan were keeping the appointment he had heard them make in the morning.

Now, although it was too far off for him to hear the voices, sharp as his ears were, it was not too far for him to distinguish the figures of the speakers. At a glance he recognized Martha as his benefactress at the cottage in the woods. Martha had been strangely kind to the boy, and he had not met with so much kindness in the world that his stock of gratitude was near the lees. Her presence on the shore, her departure in the boat, coupled with the conversation he had been allowed to hear in the morning, were premises enough for his rough logic to conclude that she was the person to be sent to the plantations. Now although he did not quite know what "the plantations" meant, he was quite well aware that it meant something which nobody would undergo by choice and preference, and he accordingly made up his mind to visit the lugger, ascertain the truth of his surmises, and, in case of their correctness, give his friend to understand what danger she was in. He was so lost in this cogitation, that he did not hear Christopher's step until he was close upon him, and then scrambled to his feet only just in time to receive the stinging punishment of his want of vigilance across his shoulders.

I have said that this poor neglected thing had not met with so much kindness as to have made any perceptible diminution of his stock of gratitude. Of his vindictiveness, on the other hand, a friendless life among a rough people made almost daily exercise. But Christopher's blow did not rankle the less on that account, for whereas gratitude is like a photograph, sensibly enfeebled by every exposure to the sun and air, revenge, like a good oil painting, only deepens and grows richer by age. That blow of Christopher's, as with a single stroke of the brush, produced a fine Rembrandtish effect in the boy's gallery of wrongs-to-be-avenged; and you may depend on it, that mental Rembrandt will, like its actual brothers on the canvas, only grow more costly by keeping.

Bad critic as he was, I don't think Christopher would have failed to see how full of deep meaning was the picture he had assisted to hang in the gallery of that young scapegrace's brain.

It was late before Denzil reached Tresellan.

He found Emma sitting before the library fire when he entered.

"What, sitting up so late, Nem?"

"I wanted to see you before I went to bed. Where have you been so long?"

"Down at Pentowan's."

"Then I fear I am too late!"

"Too late for what, Nem?"

"Why you see I have been thinking over what has been done, and it seems to me that you had by far better keep that forged bill."

"Only just come to that decision?"

"No, not exactly. It has always seemed to me the only prudent and safe course, but I have not been able to see my way to its accomplishment until now."

"And now?"

"Why now it strikes me, that as Pentowan's share in this was very small—if any; for he has nothing to show for it, and he may possibly only be romancing, and Frank's story correct, that the old priest had died and left no papers: all this considered, I say, the most natural thing for you to do in the world would be to refuse to give up this bill without having received any sort of equivalent. By this you ensure the lawyer's silence for ever; and taking it into consideration that he is a lawyer, it is prudent to have a tighter hold on him than he has on you."

"Well, I will take your advice, Nem. I shall not get off the bargain though without difficulty. Pentowan is to come to-morrow afternoon for it."

"And now I have something else to add. Aubyn, I am told, is stopping at Pentowan's!"

Denzil started and turned pale.

"That looks cursedly ugly! By Heaven, he *shan't* have the bill now!"

"You suspect——"

"What I have had a lurking fear of for some time. This lawyer *has* got the priest's papers! It would be paying his experience of dirty work and sharp practice a poor compliment to suppose that he does not see that *I* must see how desirable it is that I should keep the bill. He keeps the packet and Aubyn close at hand to use as a last resource, if he can get the forgery from me at no lower price."

"But why? If he had brought you the packet at first, the exchange would have been made, and——"

"Pshaw, child! don't you see he wants to see how cheap he can get the bill; he begins by bidding low, and will count it a capital bargain if he can purchase it for anything short of the surrender of the priest's papers. He has studied the law too long not to know that when once you have an advantage you should not let go of it until you are quite certain that by so doing you ensure a greater one."

"Well, we shall see. Good night, dear Denzil!"

"Good night, Nem!"

And so this precious pair parted on the night before their wedding.

What nice settlements were these they had been, as it were, signing! What joint partnership in guile, and sin, and shame, they had just drawn up the articles of. What a wedding, in short! With no rag of respect left on either side, and with love only on one—and that love but a base counterfeit of the true feeling at the best. Love is like certain plants that are the improved and civilized forms of mere weeds. They only flourish to perfection in a good and well-kept soil. Transplanted back to poor and overrun earth, they return to their wild state and original worthlessness, and retain only the name of their higher estate. So love, purified and tended by virtue, is a holy growth of the heart. Struggling for existence in a bosom filled with evil thoughts and disgraceful memories, it lapses into a coarse and degraded passion, an unwholesome bramble that wounds the hand which gathers it.

CHAPTER XXI.

Γάμος ἄγαμος, νύμφη ἄνυμφος.

THERE was a good steady rain falling on the day that Denzil and Emma were married. Though they both of them looked solemn and grave enough for a funeral, the ceremony in which they were engaged was a wedding. So if the old saying,

> "Happy is the corpse that the rain rains on,
> And happy is the bride that the sun shines on!"

implies the reverse of happiness to them under the altered circumstances of being respectively a be-showered bride and a sunlit corpse, why then Emma's marriage was not lacking in ill omen.

My lady-readers (if I have any left persevering enough to continue the perusal of a novel in which all the love-making and millinery are omitted, of "malice aforethought,") must not expect me to break through my rule for the sake of describing this very unpretending ceremonial.

That very necessary and conscientious institution, Jenkins, whom "Punch" so unworthily persecuted, could have made nothing of a "marriage in high life" so barren of interest. The bride was not "attired" in anything that the most prolix pen could make a line of. Sterrup was not "assisted by the Rev. ——, the brother of the bride," and half a dozen other ecclesiastical joiners. No, not the most florid penny-a-liner could have done much to improve the occasion on which "Emma, daughter of the late Ernest Rewth, Esq., J.P., of Menaduloe, in the county of Cornwall, was led to the hymeneal altar by Sir Denzil, only son and heir-at-law of the late Sir Abel Tresellan, Bart. and J. P. of Tresellan, in the same county."

To spare you conjectures as to who sustained the various parts in this miserable matrimonial farce, I may as well state that Christopher gave away the bride, and that Aunt Deborah represented the bridesmaids as efficiently as a widow twice-removed from single blessedness could do. For she had vindicated woman's supremacy over two of the other sex, who were convinced we will hope by this time, after respectively seven and ten years' repose in Devonshire churchyards, that there *were* such things as peace and silence.

Denzil had no "best-man," unless it was the clerk who held his hat and gloves while he fumbled for the ring. As Zachariah Vercoe was "an honest man and leal," he was, of the two, undoubtedly the best man in one sense—and was the best man for Denzil in another also, as the chief constable and thief-taker of the very enlightened town of Polvadnick.

It is not the slightest use, my dear reader, to become impatient with me for dancing round this portion of my story, like a shying horse capering at a dab-wash fluttering at the road-side. The fact is, I have a scruple about assisting, even as a reporter, in such an ugly business as bigamy.

Suppose, then, we imagine the knot tied and the bride kissed, and the book signed! Sterrup retires to the "Ship" to diminish his fees by a bumper to the head of Tresellan and his bride. Vercoe goes to the town hall to keep an appointment with the captain of the detachment there quartered. The Polvadnick public, which had clattered into church to see the ceremony, bringing with it a strong odour of brine, dried fish, and pitch, separated, without much conversation or discussion, to its various occupations, for it did not trouble itself further about the marriage than to say, "No Tresellan ever was wed like that before."

And it was true—arches had been built over all the roads, tables had been spread in the market-place, and cider barrels tilted at the doors of the inns at all previous Tresellan weddings. And the people had shouted and cheered, and danced, and drank the health of the happy pair till "all was blue" overhead with the growing light of the morning.

But, whether really out of respect for Sir Abel's memory, or from a lurking scruple about making rejoicings over an unmistakeable transgression of human and Divine law, Denzil had given out that, as the wedding was appointed so soon after his father's death, only for insurmountable and overpowering private reasons, he should refrain from making any of the usual preparations for the occasion.

So as no barrels were unheaded outside the inns, and no tables laid in the market-place, the people did not drink, dance, or cheer, but having stared their fill in the church, separated and went on their several avocations.

It was not the custom in the days of which I write, at all events in this remote part of England, to fly the country immediately on marriage, as forgers and other criminals do on detection. Emma and Denzil returned to Tresellan to take up their residence there from that time forth.

Aunt Deborah, who had been retained almost by brute force for the last three days, and whose boxes, ready packed, were waiting in the hall, as the party went to church, was whisked away from Tresellan gates in a post-chaise without waiting to enter the house to change the white shawl she had donned as a concession to Hymen, whom, with this one exception, it was not attempted to propitiate by the wearing of befitting garments.

Aunt Deborah, as I have said, had been twice married, so perhaps knew from experience more extensive than usual, what a very dismal thing a wedding day is. But she moreover had a family of sixteen sons and daughters, whom she had left at her house in Devon, and who had all, as was usual when left together by their mother for more than twenty-four hours, fallen out with one another furiously. No wonder the good lady was very anxious to put an end to the civil war which she knew was raging so furiously.

"Lady-bird, lady-bird,
Fly away home,
Your house is on fire
And your children at home."

So Denzil and Emma were left alone, with all Tresellan before them, where to choose their place for spending their honeymoon. It was rather depressing even to a newly-married pair. Denzil leaned his nose against the window until the top contracted a livid flatness that did not enhance its beauty. Meanwhile he drummed the "Dead March in Saul," or some such melancholy air on the glass with his finger-nails, as he watched the rain-drops trickling deviously down the pane, or tried how many he could count before some more than ordinarily large one, hanging from the frame, would fall. He was glad of any refuge from his thoughts—the present—and his wife.

She, poor mortal, having now obtained the ambition and aim of a lifetime, was just about as miserable as people generally are when the toys they have been crying for are at last given to them.

Under these circumstances Denzil was not at all sorry when it was announced to him that Mr. Pentowan was waiting to see him in the library.

He found Christopher with his back to the fire, standing as an Englishman is fond of standing, with a coat tail under each arm, and his feet about a yard apart. The meeting was not a very warm one, though abundantly courteous. It was rather after the fashion of those flourishing preludes to small-sword encounters that the skilful fencers of that day were wont to perform with all the gravity in the world. But just as all these bowings and scrapings and measurings of distance eventually gave place to the real thrust and parry business, so the civilities of our two worthies were at last swept away before the real business of the interview.

"Well, Mr. Denzil—Sir Denzil, I ask pardon—and now let us at once perform all that remains to be done with regard to our contract."

"Don't you think, Mr. Pentowan, things are best as they are?"

"Certainly, with one exception, nothing could be more satisfactory than the present position of affairs."

"That exception being——?"

"The bill. Will you have the goodness to give it to me?"

"It is not in my power to do so!"

The lawyer turned rather red at this, and felt a sense of uncomfortableness creeping over him.

"Where is it? What have you done with it?"

"I burnt it!"

"Sir Denzil Tresellan, there are some subjects

on which it is well not to jest. You echo my words used in explaining the fate of Father Seraphicus's packet. For the measure I adopted I had full and sufficient reasons. There were a hundred accidents which might have led to the discovery of that packet. That packet once discovered, all the ingenuity which you are exercising to debar me from what I have fairly earned, would have been utterly powerless to procure for you that fruition of your hopes and aspirations, which my simple act has so abundantly ensured to you. Had any consideration of self been allowed to dictate my line of conduct, I should have preferred to keep the packet at the risk of its discovery, and of the thorough frustration of your plans, instead of making you safe, and trusting to your honour to indemnify me for my generosity in destroying the evidence and insurance of my claim."

"Mr. Pentowan perhaps forgets that he is not addressing a jury for the defence, but confabulating with a *particeps criminis*."

"You may sneer, Mr. Denzil, but your scorn is not half so great as my contempt for your mean subterfuge."

Christopher took an angry march up the library and back.

"Give me the bill!" he repeated, as he returned to his former post in front of Denzil.

"I have burnt it."

"What evidence is there to prove that? Why should I believe it?"

"Had we not better exchange tinder, Mr. Pentowan? It is all the evidence either of us can bring of the destruction of that which the other so ardently desires the possession of."

"This is trifling, sir! Once for all, do you intend to withhold that which I have twice over purchased of you by acts which it is as much shame for you to exact as for me to perform."

"Don't let us grow warm in discussing the question—or thirsty either," and Denzil took out of a cupboard, the door of which was painted to simulate a book-case, a tall shapely bottle of claret.

Angry as Christopher was, he yet retained sense enough not to refuse the offer of a glass of claret of the vintage that Sir Abel had loved. Plenty of those slim flasks, ay, and of good round-sided bottles of port and sherry, had the worthy baronet and justice of the peace here committed to sawdust, hoping some day to recall them to life. Strange vicissitudes of mankind! We lay down—with what infinite care lest we crack them and spill the divine liquor!—dozen on dozen of "comet" wine, and '24 or '34 wine, and before the industrious spider has spun a veil over the resting-place of the fluid—before the first maggot has had time to pass its brief pupa existence in the sawdust—before the first fungoid efflorescence has gathered about the corks—lo! we ourselves are taken in hand by the relentless cellarer Death, who pops us into bin B or bin C, and shakes the mould over us. The brittlest of black bottles is often longer lived than we are, and not seldom is it that the stock of that particular vintage we laid such store by, calculating so nicely when we should open on it, is in prime condition and very popular when we are forgotten, and should not be by any means so pleasant to open on as that rare old pipe.

The influence of the claret on our friends was most beneficent. From very high words they came to at least outward calmness and deliberation. But however outwardly placid and agreeable their relations were, there was a decided breach between the two, and each had determined to fight to the last.

This was not *écarté*-playing now. As I hinted before, it was fencing—and with "unbated points." At last both combatants grew weary, and called "a bout"—there were no hits on either side to score yet.

"Till to-morrow, Sir Denzil, I take my leave. Till to-morrow. Then all must and shall be decided. You may possibly wish to consult your wife, as you are a Benedict now, so I will give you ample time for consideration and discussion. I have no wish to press you or hurry you. So—until to-morrow! Courtesy has been my bane through life. Good bye!"

Christopher little knew that not only had Denzil consulted his wife, but was positively acting on her directions, or he would not have chuckled to himself at what he had said on that head.

"Egad," he fancied, "that was neat. He'll think that I mean it for a threat that I will tell his wife the odd things I have to reveal!"

So musing to himself our rogue strode away to the ferry, trying to persuade himself to keep a light heart and a sure trust in his ultimate victory over Denzil.

But somehow there was a cloud hanging over him that he could not shake off—a shadow of coming evil that he vainly endeavoured to pierce or to explain away.

CHAPTER XXII.

IN THE FRYING-PAN.

THE "Flying Spray" was safely berthed in a little pool known to the fishermen of this part of the coast as "The Frying Pan." The reason of the name was obvious. A deep channel cut by some old geologic disturbance between upright walls of rock on either hand, and narrow, although deep and not very straight, formed a rude resemblance to the handle of the familiar cooking implement. The pan itself was represented by the channel in question, widening at its termination into a sheet of water, affording sufficient room for a vessel of greater length than the lugger to lie in comfortably, and even to be turned round in, by careful warping.

This snug natural harbour had the advantage of becoming invisible to an eye unaccustomed to the coast, at a distance of barely a quarter of a mile from the shore. Its mouth seemed no more than a rather more marked indentation of the irregular face of the cliff than usual, while a high reef of rocks, which formed a sort of natural breakwater at its entrance, concealed from sight what would otherwise have betrayed its whereabouts, the existence of a creek of water running into the cleavage of the line of coast.

It says much for the *esprit de corps* of the body politic of smugglers that this quiet retreat was so well-kept a secret. It says much, too, for the easy virtue of the inhabitants of this seaboard, who clearly were not vigorous upholders of, or believers in, the justice of the prohibitory customs' laws.

It also, I fancy, does *not* say much either for the vigilance or the probity of the guardians of those laws. I have been told that the 'longshore watchers about here were actually in the pay of the smugglers. You must remember that this smuggling was, in the days of which I write, a favourite sort of gambling investment with the better classes—with the well-to-do farmers and the landed proprietors along the coast. As these loyal subjects, good men and true, grand jurors, and petty justices, had a good deal to do with the appointment of the coast-guard of the period, it was very easy for them to employ for that service men whose views of their duty would not compel them to interfere with the interests of their patrons—nay, indeed, would allow them to assist in running a cargo when the weather was favourable and hands short.

No wonder that the folk of the sea-board had cosy little balances at their bankers, or that their wives were noticeable for excellent silk gowns and choice laces and gloves.

On the dull morning of Denzil's wedding-day you may be sure Martha was not sorry to have the monotony of the slow-going hours enlivened by the appearance of her ragged young *protégé*, who came on board tolerably early. The chief part of the lugger's crew were gone to Polvadnick, some to stare at the wedding, some to drink at the "Ship," some to hang about the town-hall for scraps of intelligence as to the movements of the soldiers, and some to vend under cover of a cartload of pilchards those prohibited articles of trade, which human nature, with characteristic perversity, was all the more inclined to buy because they were contraband.

Martha and the boy therefore were not interfered with. The watch amused themselves with smoking or fishing. Bowser was curled up in the bows with his books, making out his debtor and creditor account for the information of his employers.

"So this was the sort of thing with which you employed yourself on foggy days when you stayed away from the cottage?"

The boy nodded, and then looking round to make sure no one was watching him, asked, "I say, I saw you with Mas'r Denzil last night. What's he to you?"

"My husband, child, that's all!"

"Do you know he's sending you off to the plantations?"

"Nonsense! what can you have got into your silly head?"

"Yes, he is—and he's married to-day to Miss Emma, his cousin."

Martha sprang to her feet; and it was only by the exercise of great self-restraint that she stifled a cry of surprise.

"Oh, it's all true," continued her informant, "I heard it all planned between Lawyer Pentowan and the skipper yonder; and you're to be got out of the way and shipped to some place called the plantations. I've been told it's a nasty country to go to, so I thought I'd tell you."

"Denzil married!" muttered Martha to herself. The boy caught up the word.

"Married! Ay, safe and sure by this time. I saw Zakky Varcoe goin' up to Parson Sterrup as I came away, and the parson's bands was out to dry in the garden as I passed by it to the bridge-end."

"I must go on shore at once."

"The skipper won't let you, I fancy. Can you write?"

"Yes," said Martha, smiling at the abruptness of the query.

"Well, you write and ask Lawyer Pentowan to send for you?"

"I shall be just as far off my object as I am now, I'm afraid."

"Well, you go and try the skipper; only tell him you want to go on shore to get something, or he'll guess I've been 'peaching. He won't let you go though, I'll warrant."

And the boy was right. Bowser, roused from his calculations, gave a tolerably courteous but very decided refusal to let Martha leave the ship. "He was only to do so on receiving a given token from Christopher Pentowan."

"If I send a letter to him——"

"Who's to take it?"

"Oh, any one—perhaps you will send the boy there," and Martha pointed to the urchin, who was hanging over the bulwark apparently intent on watching one of the crew fishing.

"Well, I'm an obliging fellow, and can't say no. Here, young imp of sin!" he shouted; "come to the lady here!" The boy came aft, and received his orders. Martha wrote a brief note to the lawyer, the direction of which Bowser inspected to make sure that it was addressed to the right person. With this in the crown of his ragged cap, Martha's *protégé* scrambled out along the bowsprit, and dropped on to the green sward of the shore, over which it projected. In five minutes more he was on the moors hastening towards Polvadnick with all the speed he could muster, which was no contemptible amount, and with all his rags fluttering in the wind, as if he had been a scarecrow running against time.

Left to herself, Martha's feelings were anything but enviable. In Christopher she had placed no great reliance, but had yet believed that for his own interest as well as hers, he would not have allowed Denzil to go so far as actually to marry his cousin. According to what he had told her, he was to have insisted on getting the forgery into his possession before the day was fixed for the marriage, on pain of revealing the existence of Martha to Emma. That bill once in his hands, the lawyer could have dictated his own terms, amongst which he had agreed to insist on the acknowledgment of Martha, who in return had promised him all the advantages which her power over Denzil could procure for him.

But Martha did not know the whole truth of Denzil's plot to obtain the Tresellan property, and she was quite ignorant of one thing—the knowledge Emma had of that plot—a knowledge which placed Denzil as much in her power as he was in that of his wife or the lawyer.

Perhaps, too, Martha was weak enough to believe what Christopher had been cunning enough to lead her to suppose, without actually saying it, in so many words (which would probably not have persuaded Martha of his sincerity so effectually), —namely, that he still retained some sparks of his old love to her, or at least was willing to make what reparation he could, late though it was, for the injury he had inflicted on her.

Upon my word, Christopher must have been a consummate rogue to succeed in twice deceiving a woman of such a nature as Martha's was. In doing so the second time, however, Christopher had succeeded in ensuring to himself a hate that would be satisfied with nothing less than his death.

That he had deceived her the first time, Martha looked upon as a natural contingency of the relations of a man and woman. The only person she had not forgiven for that early error was herself, not Christopher, and the thing she could not bring herself to pardon was her folly of letting herself be duped, not the, to her inevitable ingredient in his connection with her—his crime of duping her.

So noon came and passed, and Martha still stretched her gaze across the pool to the pathway along which the boy had disappeared. One by one the stragglers returned from Polvadnick, and were received and closely questioned by Bowser, who had at last finished balancing his accounts, which showed him very satisfactorily that within the last six months he had brought over a thousand pounds clear profit to his employers.

CHAPTER XXIII.

WHAT MAKES THE WORLD GO ROUND.

On the same evening that Christopher accompanied Denzil to St. Erdan's Cove, Aubyn and Lucinda found themselves alone together in the garden for the first time.

Those of my readers who have retentive memories will recall the fact that, when in an early chapter we found Aubyn looking down on Polvadnick from the cliff above the ferry, his eyes at last rested on Christopher's house. It was a truth which at that time he had not confessed to himself, but none the less a truth on that account, that Aubyn admired Lucinda. Troth-plight to Emma, his honourable soul would have shrunk from contemplating the possibility of being unfaithful, even in thought, to her. It is likely that had he married his cousin, only on his deathbed, when doubts are resolved, and the thoughts of the heart reveal themselves, would Sir Aubyn Tresellan of Tresellan have acknowledged to himself that his love had never belonged to the mother of his children, but had silently enshrined another image in his heart, and worshipped it with the insensible and mute devotion of a lifetime.

But now all this would never be. Whatever else might be, that could never be. He was free and unfettered to own the passion that had filled his heart from his boyish days. Free! but to do what? To offer to a young and beautiful girl who had never known a day's care, anxiety, or sorrow, the reversion of a ruined man's affection —the share of an outcast's only birthright— shame, poverty, and neglect.

Such were the burning thoughts that coursed through this poor fellow's brain as he walked by Lucinda's side along the garden paths, dappled with light and shade. Under the sea wall the clear wave kept up its monotonous song, lapping at the weed-hung stakes, and lit up by myriad points of light as each ripple of the rising tide spent itself against the barrier.

The same soft influence of the hour, and the placid moonlit scene, which revived the tenderness in even Denzil's heart, stirred the breast of Aubyn to its inmost depths. Nor was Lucinda exempted from the potent sway of midnight and silence.

Let us step aside reverently, my friends, from

this dew-jewelled lawn, and not intrude on the delicious tortures these two young people were undergoing. There was something too noble to be made a spectacle of in Aubyn's struggle to resist the mighty impulse which urged him to lay all his wealth of devotion (alas! all the wealth he now possessed) at Lucinda's feet, to find in exchange for it the love, the pity, the sympathy, for which his soul yearned, and without which his life was but a dull and tardy pilgrimage across a desert—a pilgrimage whose goal was the grave. Those among us who have tender hearts will gladly withdraw and leave these two lovers to reveal their feelings to each other—to prattle that artless talk which at some time or another we have all of us thought such delightful wisdom, such a language of the soul!

Then and there did Aubyn confess his long affection, and then and there did Lucinda in her queenly way receive the homage, and confess how dear it was to her.

Happy time! golden season of life! Why cannot existence be made to consist of one unending declaration of love? Never does earth seem so lovely and so loveable—never does heaven seem so near and beneficent, as when we look upon them with eyes that have but just read in another's looks the first bright lesson of reciprocated affection.

Larks never sang so sweetly, nightingales never complained with so delicious a melancholy—roses never scattered so abundant a largesse of perfume—jessamines never blossomed into such constellations of odorous star-flowers—limes never hummed with such melodious bees—larches never waved such spicy fragrance from their graceful tasselled branches—turf never yielded so softly and springily to the tread—sky never revealed such depths of azure, or breathed such gentle breezes—as on the day when you or I heard the first whisper of love!

"See Naples—and then die!" Rather learn that you are loved for the first time, and then close your eyes—fold your hands—and turn to your last sleep. There shall never be light like it again on your path—there shall never be music like it again in your ear!

Hear the first whisper of love, and then to sleep! say I, and that speedily, for love is the veriest bubble that ever gleamed with the opalescent hues of the rainbow! It is like the disentombed body of Heloise, whose grave was opened by some curious monks, graduates doubtless in that mystery of which she was high priestess and martyr. Fairer than anything that life had ever possessed of beauty was that calm dead face. Under the lids, white and translucent as ivory, the blue eyes seemed to show, as though it only needed the voice of Abelard to make them open. Faint as the reflex on a lily's leaves of some neighbouring rose's blushes was the bloom on the soft cheek, and about the lips, that had so often sealed on those of her lover the vows that were stronger than duty, than honour, than life, than death itself, still glowed so perfect a sweetness that the youngest of the four monks bent over to kiss them. A touch! and that surpassing beautiful image had crumbled, and in the coffin was only dust with a few shreds of black serge. Such, so sudden and so mysterious, is the conversion of love's golden fruit into a handful of bitter ashes at the first touch of the world's reality!

Not that all love is thus brief and transitory. It is only the unalloyed metal that melts thus—only the most delicate-bloomed fruit that perishes so. There is a plenty of apples, ay, and of turnips, that will do for every-day fare, and do not vanish at the first impact of a tooth.

Gracious powers! into what a rhapsody have I been misled; all the while protesting that I would shun this love scene and its protestations of affection.

Well! if you must know, I have served your curiosity the same trick that the peewit plays off on the boy who passes too near her nest.

With a lamed wing and plaintive cry, I have induced you to follow me away from the too close proximity you had gained to these palpitating trembling young birds of mine, nestling side by side in the arbour under the south wall.

Now that the declarations are all over, I smooth my ruffled feathers and laugh at you, as I fly back to my pair of lovers. But another time, don't be taken in when I begin to rave in this way, on a subject of which I solemnly protest to you I am as profoundly ignorant as the phœnix—which, being the sole individual of the species that ever existed, may be fairly supposed to have had no experience of the tender passion!

Thank goodness, by the time we return to Aubyn and Lucinda, all the avowal "business" is over, as they would say on the stage. The latter has explained to our hero the history of the plot against him, from the moment of her overhearing Denzil and her father concocting their villany in the office, down to the present time—

though of course the information she had to give him for the period after old Gregory's departure was but meagre.

Aubyn was horrified at the refinement of wickedness thus revealed to him. His whole nature revolted, his reason trembled before the contemplation, and for a time his better angel fled, and his heart was filled with black and savage thoughts.

"They have made an Ishmael of me!" he burst out; "and they shall find that my hand is against every man's—as every man's hand is against me."

He turned to Lucinda almost fiercely. "Miss Pentowan, the noble efforts you made to preserve me from these fiendish plans is the one thing which saves me from an entire disbelief in human nature—almost a disbelief in heaven. For that I owe you a debt of gratitude that a score of lives were too short to repay. For the love I have been betrayed into revealing,—it should have died and been buried with me—for what right have *I*, a wretch without a hope in the world, to dare to breathe it to you? Forget it, I beseech you; and hereafter, when you learn my death—that is, if the world takes the trouble to report so unimportant a thing—think of me as one who in his last moments remembered only you and your kindness, and died blessing your name."

Before she had time to reply he was gone.

As she turned down the path by the bleaching lawn, to enter the house unobserved, by the side door, she saw a light come into the room Aubyn occupied. It was he, but his actions were so wild that she could not but pause to watch him, fearful lest he should attempt some desperate act.

Her horror and apprehension were not allayed when she saw him take from his valise a pair of pistols, examine them, and finally load them.

While she hesitated whether to cry out to him, or to rush indoors and raise an alarm, she saw him turn round as if listening to some sound in the house. To her immense relief she heard her father's voice calling on Aubyn to descend and speak to him for a few moments, if he had not retired to rest.

The lawyer had just returned from the Cove of St. Erdan, and his object was to obtain a promise from Aubyn that he would not leave Polvadnick without giving him notice of his intention. For Christopher felt the profound necessity of having him at hand to use against Denzil in case of necessity.

No sooner had Aubyn descended than Lucinda hastened into the house. With a rapid but noiseless step she mounted to his room, and by the light of the moon made her way to the table where the pistols lay. Emma, with all her nerve, would have feared to touch those weapons, but there was no such weakness about Lucinda. She had seen her father load and unload his brace often, and was familiar with the sight of them. With a steady hand, and without a single mistake, though it was for the first time in her life, she unscrewed the barrels, removed the bullets, screwed the barrels on again, and then throwing the balls out of the window, crept to her own room, and there on her knees sought the strength and council she so deeply needed in the new and trying position in which she found herself placed between her love for Aubyn and her natural affection for her father.

CHAPTER XXIV.

CONFOUND YOU, SIR, YOU'RE ALWAYS TYING YOUR SHOE.

THERE is a very good story told of a young undergraduate, who rushed out of the Schools at Oxford after having been subjected by a long and tedious process to the torture which is now-a-days called "ploughing," but which I should be inclined to describe as harrowing. Boiling over with indignation and spleen, which he could not vent on his reverend inquisitors, he rushed into the Schools' quad to find a sedate and respectable citizen busily engaged in the re-adjustment of a deranged bootlace. To rush up to this unconscious individual, seize him by the throat, and shake him until he had scarce breath enough left in his body to convey his inquiry as to the reason of this violence, was the work of a few seconds. Then, somewhat recovering his reason, as his rage escaped by this novel safety-valve, the collegian in reply to the expostulations of his victim gave the following explanation, which, inasmuch as it was spontaneous and immediate, we may suppose to be the real conclusion of the rude yet forcible logic of nature.

"Confound you, sir, you're *always* tying your shoe!"

There is nothing witty in the story—nothing eminently comic—indeed, its only approach to wit is to that lowest order of fun, the practical joke. Yet I never heard that story told without its eliciting a universal and unanimously favourable verdict from those who heard—even though it was for the hundredth time.

The reason is, that the story is so profoundly true and natural! The heart at once acknowledges it, and feels that it is a thing which could only be related because it actually occurred—not because it was invented by the most ingenious and happy humourist that ever set a good jest a-going.

It is not so long since the world saw an instance of this in a great republic, which, finding itself unable to repress aspirations for freedom, which it was pleased to call a rebellion, found an outlet for its rage in a stream of abuse poured upon a country which had studiously held aloof from the contest with the most blameless neutrality.

"Confound you," said the vixenish commonwealth, finding a voice in the columns of a scurrilous press—"Confound you, you are always tying your shoe!"

Now Christopher's rage at Denzil's line of conduct, when he left Tresellan after the interview described a chapter ago, had reached what I may describe as the shoe-string stage. He and his adversary were encamped and inactive. A Potomac of claret had flowed between their hostile armaments, and each, outwardly calm and seemingly certain of victory, was internally perplexed as to the way to that desirable consummation.

Christopher, his first burst of anger and disgust over, grew particularly cautious not to offend Denzil and defy him to a contest *à l'outrance.* So though he presented a firm, perhaps threatening front to the foe, he refrained from overt acts of hostility, calculated to incite to retaliation.

But his anger, like other eruptive disorders, checked in one place, burst out only the more virulently in another. He snapt at the butler who let him out, and who was rather too hearty and jovial, possibly in consequence of a laudable respect for the traditions of the Tresellan family. "It should go hard," he said, in the servants' hall, "before a Tresellan wedding was allowed to pass over without some one's getting drunk in honour of the occasion."

The ferryman received but a curt reply to his inquiries after Christopher's health, and the old boatmen on the beach got very stiff bows indeed in answer to their obsequious bowings and doffings of "sou'-westers."

This was some relief to Christopher; he was delighted to have the power to snub somebody. But he needed, for the full satisfaction of the shoe-string frenzy, an opportunity of inflicting more than mental pain—nothing short of a physical exercise of his rage would really calm the ebullition—just as a stir is needed to restrain a saucepan from boiling over.

It would perhaps have been an uncomfortable time for the Pentowan household—for the maid of all work and the boy who cleaned the boots and knives, at least, if not for Lucinda—but for the following circumstance.

Little Kit, whom we last saw bounding over the moors between the Frying-Pan and Polvadnick, just reached Pentowan's back garden-gate as the lawyer was laying his hand on the latch. Panting and out of breath, he could only just pant, "Stop, sir. Stop. I've something pressing."

"Well!" said Christopher, "what is it?"

But to get the note out of that complicated patchwork of rags that represented his trousers was no easy task for the boy.

Christopher was not inclined to be too patient.

"I can't wait, you young limb of Satan! Tell me what it is!"

But the lad did not answer. His whole attention was taken up by the care requisite to pilot Martha's triangular billet through the rents and patches of his pocket. Just as it reached the light, ill-luck would have it that the threads of a "gobble-stitch" that our urchin had planted there to keep body and soul of the garment together should catch it and jerk it from between his fingers. Instead of falling back into the dilapidated pocket—indeed, with so many other courses before it, it would have been strange if it had returned exactly the way it came—the missive dropped between the variegated cloth of the trousers, and the damaged cobwebby fabric that still clung superstitiously where it had formerly served as lining.

Christopher with intense disgust saw the urchin make a succession of rapid grabs down his leg as the letter slid down. But it eluded all efforts at recapture, and lodged at the bottom.

With an angry "pish!" the lawyer turned to enter the gate, but the earnestness of the boy's appeal stopped him.

"Don't go, sir, only wait a minute; I'll get it now easy. It'll be a sorry day for you, sir, if you don't get the letter."

So saying the urchin broke apart the rotten stitches that still held the cloth and lining together and rescued the note.

Christopher snatched it, and breaking it open, ran his eye hurriedly over the contents.

You may easily imagine how furious they made him. In a moment he wondered what was the source from which Martha had obtained her information; for instead of cunningly getting him to give her leave to land, she, like a woman, reproached him for his treachery. But he did not wonder for more than a moment. The eagerness of the messenger, the breathless haste with which he had evidently performed the errand, the earnest attention with which he watched its result, all showed Christopher that here was the culprit. He did not stop to wonder what had induced the boy to tell Martha.

"You sneaking young spy and imp of mischief. What meddling demon set you to interfere with me?" he roared, and lifting his walking cane he struck the boy across the face with it, violently, cruelly, twice. It was a brutal action, and woke the brute passions of its victim, and no wonder. Although already half-blinded by the wheals that rose red and smarting, the urchin flew at once to the boy's armoury, a heap of stones.

Two jagged flints dinting the door close by his head, warned Christopher that it was time to retreat, and he sprang through the door, closing it after him and shooting the bolt with very undignified haste. Nor did he loiter in the garden, for after a few good-sized pebbles had bounded over the wall and rolled along the path at his heels, Christopher heard a scrambling sound on the door which announced that the infuriated young animal was attempting to climb the walls. By the time he had done so, Christopher was safe indoors.

So the boy, after indulging in the impotent satisfaction of grinning and shaking his fist at the house, jumped down again, and going to the water-side bathed his burning face in the brine. His first impulse was to break the lawyer's windows, but he had a wholesome fear of Constable Vercoe and the lock-up that stood by the pound. And besides, there was his friend "the lady," to be considered. There was no time to run back and consult with her; for it was just beginning to grow dusk, and the "Flying Spray" was to sail as soon as it was dark.

The reason of this change, the news of which Kit had learned from one of the crew whom he met on his way to Polvadnick, was that in connection with the detachment of the troops from Plymouth was the sending of several boat-crews and a company of marines to make a descent along the coast. The plan was well-conceived. As the soldiers arrived, the smugglers would bolt like so many rats, and be off to sea, only to fall into the hands of the cruising expedition. But no plans, however well conceived, are of any use to ensnare those who are fully posted in all their particulars. One of the part owners of the "Flying Spray" was the paymaster of the Marines; and who but he should send a mounted messenger with a letter to his partners to warn them of the coming danger. The letter was directed to Bowser at Christopher's; but as the second in command, Stimpson, was on the spot he opened it.

You may be sure he was soon making a tour of the town, picking up all stragglers in the various inns, and sending them off post haste to the "Frying-Pan."

Kit saw there was no time to be lost; but he rightly considered a few minutes spent in considering what was best to be done was not lost time.

Any one who had seen him curled up in the bows of one of the beached boats, would have thought him asleep, but he was far from that.

Of course the obvious thing to be done was to tell the officer in command of the troops of the whereabouts of the lugger. But it was a decided step for this poor wretch to take. He was an outcast with no friends in the world, and no livelihood save the scraps he could pick from the gutter, until he obtained employ in the service of Bowser, who found in him a tool at once useful and unsuspected.

But to do the boy and Nature credit (for there was nothing else involved in the proceeding), he resolved to give up all for the sake of his benefactress, much more readily than a civilized and educated being might have done. Indeed, his delay in coming to the determination rose chiefly from the time he spent in devising how he should save Bowser also, whom he considered a benefactor too, from the results of the lugger's capture.

You see how cheaply Martha and Bowser bought this lad's devotion and gratitude. The one had incidentally been of use to him in seeking amusement and distraction in an idle hour; the other had paid him a pittance for doing what he could find no other to perform better, or indeed so well.

Having at last made up his mind, Kit rose and walked into the town. He loitered about the door of the town-hall until he made sure no one was observing him, and then ducking past the sentry, who was beguiling his time with a stealthy whistle, he dived into the building. He had not got far before he was "brought up all-standing" by the halberd of the sergeant, who had just reached the door of the council-room (in which the officer had taken up his quarters) to make a report.

An altercation ensued. The sergeant would not let the boy enter; indeed, would have him turned out unless he told his errand. The boy, who knew how many spies were employed by Bowser everywhere, thought his secret the safer the fewer people knew it.

The noise of the parley, which finished by a scuffle as the sergeant began to push the urchin down the stairs, called out the officer. Seeing the marks of Christopher's blows on the boy's face, he was inclined to believe that the soldier had been ill-using him; and as of all things he wished to stand well with the townsfolk, he sternly ordered the sergeant to leave the lad alone.

No sooner was that worthy's hand off him, than Kit was up the three stairs he had been forced down, in a twinkling, and shot into the room, past the officer who followed him in more slowly, and not without some wonder at his wild conduct.

As I am uncertain whether some of my readers may not possibly be in the interest of Captain Bowser, I shall wait outside the council room door and not report the interview which took place.

But I can inform you of what I can see from that post. I see the sergeant recalled. I see one of the soldiers, who had once served in a man-of-war, summoned. If I look from the side window of the hall I shall see him go down to the water's edge, hire a boat and two fishermen, and put away to sea. If I were on the beach I should overhear the fishermen laughing at the idea of the "sojer" going fishing, as he tells them he is, at that time of night. "He'd need row fast if he means to reach the whiting ground before dark," they say. And he is rowing fast; the aspen staves bend at every stroke, and the boat leaps from crest to crest of a short sea, as if life depended on its speed.

CHAPTER XXV.

OUT OF THE FRYING-PAN INTO THE FIRE.

At about seven o'clock, when it was quite dusk, the officer and the sergeant came out of the council room together; took four men with loaded firelocks with them, and marched towards lawyer Pentowan's. So I will leave my seat by the council room door and follow.

Leaving his men in the doorway of the next house, the officer goes alone to Christopher's door and knocks. The servant opens the door, and he asks to see her master; "the officer of the detachment at the town hall sends his compliments, and will Mr. Pentowan draw up a warrant for him."

As he gives the message he slips his half-pike into the opening of the door and whistles. The men dart from their hiding-place, and before the girl has time to scream, they fling open the door of the parlour, and the captain lays his hand on the lawyer's shoulder, and arrests him "In the king's name."

Christopher turns pale, but his presence of mind does not forsake him. He asks to see the officer's warrant.

"I have a general warrant to apprehend smugglers," is the conclusive answer.

Christopher ground his teeth with rage. Here was a thunder-clap, just when he thought the glass pointed to "set fair." For when he came into the house after leaving Kit in such haste, he found a note from Stimpson, in which he read that the lugger would sail in a few hours. So he was quite at rest about Martha's future, and felt sure it would be long ere he received another letter from her.

Poor Lucinda was in sad distress, and as the door closed behind her father, she sat down and wept as if her heart would break. And what was worst of all was that she could not fly to Aubyn for advice and counsel. He had left the house about half an hour previously. It was late and dark, so that few people saw the lawyer marched off to the town hall. Of course the affair got wind, and was talked of, but as the smuggler's crew had all left the town, you remember, the "Flying Spray" was not favoured with the intelligence of Pentowan's arrest.

As he entered the town hall, that worthy was

aware of Kit's presence, and at once recognized his betrayer in him. Kit grinned and pointed to his disfigured face, then turning to the officer, said, "I want you to promise me something."

"You shall have the full reward, my brave fellow."

"Thank you, captain; but I want a little thing beside that."

"What is it?"

"The loan of that ring on lawyer Pentowan's finger there."

In spite of his protestations Christopher had to deliver up the signet, though it was not without some hesitation that the captain trusted the ragged youngster with the jewel.

"What security have I that you will return it?"

"If I don't, buy the lawyer another—if he'll want one—with the money that's promised in the reward."

The captain laughed, and in ten minutes more Kit, ring in hand, was bounding over the moors to the Frying-Pan, like a young racer.

When he reached the lugger, the crew were busily employed in getting ready for sea. Preparations were being made to warp her out of the channel, and the anchor was a-trip. Scrambling on board along one of the booms which rested on the shore, Kit found Bowser trying to calm Martha, who, as you may guess, was in no great state of exhilaration at sight of the bustle, which announced an early departure.

Showing the ring to the captain, he told him he had orders to take Martha back with him. The captain was to leave the lugger in command of Stimpson and to go to the little cave in St. Erdan's Cove, there to wait till Christopher came and brought back Martha, and gave some further instructions for the cruise of the "Spray."

Bowser of course obeyed what he had every reason to believe were the lawyer's instructions. Stimpson took command of the lugger, and the trio landed and walked along the cliff to Polvadnick. When they reached the point above St. Erdan's Cove, Bowser dragged a rope ladder from under a boulder close by, and securing it to an iron staple, driven into the rock, and concealed from view by a clump of thorn, threw it over the edge of the cliff. He then let himself over and descended to the rock platform, about a foot in width, that projected at the entrance of the cave. This cave, known as St. Erdan's Cell, was a hole in the steep face of the cliff, and was generally believed to be inaccessible. The smugglers had, however, contrived to appropriate so useful, because so unsuspected, a lair, by having one rope ladder at the top of the cliff, as we have seen, and another in the cave itself.

When Bowser was safe down, Kit drew up the ladder. But instead of hiding it in the old place, he carried it to a shallow pool of water hard by, and hid it in the mud there. He was not sure, in the uncertainty of coming events, whether some one might not point out the usual hiding-place. Then he lay down on the extreme verge of the height, and putting his head over, called out, "Captain Bowser."

"All right, youngster!"

"The soldiers are bound to have the "Spray" to-night, so you stop where you are, and I'll come and get you off to-morrow. You'll find a barrel of biscuit and pork in the back."

"Why, odds bobs, boy! why didn't you tell me before? Here, let down the ladder, I must go back and do what I can for the old craft."

"It's no good, captain, you're bound to stop there. I've taken away the ladder."

A hasty search in the cave convinced Bowser of that. He began to rave like a caged wild-beast.

"It's all for the best, cap'n. You'll say so

yourself to-morrow, and—but hush! here's the soldiers coming, so lie still and keep quiet."

Sure enough the tramp of the soldiers reached the captain's ear as he paced up and down his prison.

Kit jumped up, and he and Martha had regained the road and were walking quietly towards the town when they met the soldiers.

Kit put the ring into the officer's hand.

"What are you doing with that petticoat there?" asked the latter.

"Why, she was going on board, but I persuaded her not; she was best out of the way."

"You're sure we are on the right track," said the other, as he hurried on again.

"You can't miss," was the answer; "a mile or a mile and a half on."

So the tramp of the marching men died away on Bowser's ear. But another regular sound, more familiar to him, took its place. It was the sound of oars in the rowlocks, and he knew at once that the stroke was a quick one. Looking out to sea he made out three or four man-of-war's boats stealing along down the coast, while out in the offing he fancied he could see a large vessel in full sail, standing in as near the coast as was safe.

"Trapped, by Jove!" was the smuggler's

exclamation, as he thought of the "Spray," and then as he recollected his own position, "So am I! Curse that 'peaching little imp!"

There was a moon this night, but the clouds quite hid it, although the rain had long ceased. So Martha and Kit did not perceive what was going on to seaward. It was only to the eye of a sailor like Bowser that that was revealed.

As they reached the last turn of the cliff-path before it dipped in front of Tresellan, they heard a report as if of a distant discharge of fire-arms.

"What is that?" asked Martha; "they can't have reached the Frying-Pan, as you call it, yet!"

"Not yet for half an hour," was her companion's answer; "and besides it didn't come from that way. It was from the moors in front there—the other side of the town."

"What can it be at this time of night, I wonder!"

"A highwayman, of course," said Kit, "there's lots of them come on the heath there; I've watched them often when I've been sleeping for a night under the peat stacks."

"Poor boy," said Martha; and the two walked on in silence.

If they had walked another half hour or so

they would have heard shots fired, and faint shouts in the other direction. The soldiers reached the "Spray's" lurking-place just as she was being warped out of the narrow gut that joined the pool with the sea. There was no time to lose. A handful of the men managed to spring on board, but the towing-party, seeing the danger the lugger was in, gave way with a will, and she was out of the channel in a very short time. The soldiers were, of course, hemmed in, and would soon have been overpowered had not a sudden diversion been created in their favour. As the soldiers sprang on board, the sergeant, who was with the rear-rank, ordered his right-hand man to discharge his piece. This was a concerted signal for the man-of-war and her boats; to fetch which down to the scene of action, and not to fish, the ex-seaman had been despatched by the officer some hours before.

At the signal, the frigate, which had laid-to a short distance from shore, discharged a gun, whose report went booming and echoing from headland to headland, and waked some of the heaviest sleepers in Tresellan in a pretty fright.

At the same moment half a dozen boats that had laid on their oars in the shade of the cliff, on either side of the creek, shot out and encircled the fated lugger.

After a brief struggle, in which six were killed and about twice that quantity wounded, the smuggler became the lawful prize of his Britannic Majesty. Her crew were bound hand and foot, and left in charge of a squad of marines, while the frigate's boats towed her under the guns of that vessel, and there anchored her till daylight.

You may guess Bowser was not highly delighted when he spied this state of affairs in the gray morning, as he peeped out of the involuntary lurking-place, where he had spent about as unpleasant a night as had ever fallen to his lot.

"Out of the frying-pan into the fire with a vengeance!" he muttered, as he turned into the cave again to take his modest breakfast of biscuit and rum and water.

CHAPTER XXVI.

SOMETHING STARTLING.

THAT same gray morning twilight which peeped in upon the sinner in the Saint's Grot, looked in at the windows of Tresellan, and woke the sleepers there. By the time the first streaks of sun, breaking through the fog, had dashed the turret of grim Old Morse with crimson, and spattered the diamond-panes with red sparks (as if for a tardy illumination in honour of Denzil's wedding), the whole of Tresellan was on the move.

Denzil had waked early enough to watch the last stars go out, and to see the various objects in the room change from strange fantastic figures into curtains, dresses, and furniture. Was it some strange foreboding of ill that had made his rest so troubled? twice he had started up in the belief that there was a hand at his throat; and very, very welcome was the daylight to him.

In the gray of the dawn the marines had marched their prisoners into Polvadnick, and the officer had sent off for Lord Trenbrase, who was the nearest justice of the peace now Sir Abel was dead.

As is generally the case, the Tresellan servants knew what was going on before their master. But they were far from learning the right version of the night's events from the people who dropped in with their little budgets of news. About Pentowan especially, the strangest stories were circulated; all as wide of the truth as might well be. "He had discovered the smugglers; he had been closeted with the officer all night; he was to bring the charge against the prisoners before Lord Trenbrase." But these rumours did not get beyond the servants' hall. Denzil and Emma were not so popular there, or so prone to encourage any confidences, as to induce any of the domestics to tell the news.

The first thing Denzil heard of what had happened was what he gathered from a note, in which "the officer in command of the detachment at Polvadnick craved permission to use the justice-hall at Tresellan, for the purpose of bringing certain smugglers, taken the previous night, before Lord Trenbrase."

You may be sure Denzil was in a fever in a moment. The smugglers taken last night could hardly be any others than those to whom Martha had been handed over. If they were brought to Tresellan, and she with them, there *must* be an explosion. He was crushed at the very thought. Then, as he turned it over in his mind, he became furious. Like a wild beast in a trap, he raged up and down, foaming at the mouth; he leaped at every plan that promised escape; only to give it up despairingly, as the brute falls back wounded and dispirited from its bounding against the bars.

It was well for him, perhaps, that Emma was not within earshot, for he raved aloud. What the "orderly" thought of his conduct we will not undertake to say, but as he stood in the hall outside the library door, awaiting an answer, he gave way to as much astonishment and curiosity as so old and tried a soldier would permit himself to indulge in while on duty.

By and by Denzil recalled himself, and penned a short note, placing Tresellan "at the officer's disposal for the ends of justice." Then he went to seek Emma, in a vague hope that she might suggest something.

As he approached the Blue Parlour he heard her singing. It was a quaint old ballad, a great favourite of Sir Abel's. As Denzil listened, he seemed to have been dreaming for this long time past, and began to think that when he opened the door he should find his father seated by the harpsicord, as was his wont, beating time on it with his fingers. The song was so sweet, that Denzil paused ere he opened the door.

"Ah, woe is me, for my old thyme's dead
And I cannot get any new—
For the place where the old thyme used to grow
Is all over-run with rue.

"Then I'll pluck up that runny, runny root,
That grows so fine and so clear,
And plant it in a steady old oak
That has stood for many a year.

"Stand you up, stand you up, you steady old oak,
And never either fade or die,
And I'll stand as true to my true love
As the stars stand true in the sky."

There was infinite tenderness in the tone of the last few lines, as Emma turned from the instrument to Denzil, who was just then opening the door. But a glance at his face soon quenched all soft thoughts.

"Why, Den, have you seen a ghost?"

"No; at least not since last night!"

"Nonsense! But what ails the man?"

"Well, they have taken the smugglers, and they are to be brought here to be tried."

"Heaven have mercy! And what then? You speak as if they were your dearest friends. What on earth is it to you if they are caught—and hanged too!"

Denzil had made a mistake. Emma was quite right to wonder at his excitement. He tried to explain it.

"Well, no! It is nothing to me—but just after our wedding to have——"

"Oh! pray don't fancy it will at all mar the effect of that brilliant ceremony."

"You are hard on me, Nem. It was obliged to be a quiet marriage."

"True, Den dear; and whatever it was in other respects, at all events it was a wedding, and we are man and wife."

"Yes, yes, of course;" and Denzil's face lengthened as he thought of Martha and her probable return, which could not but alter Emma's opinion of the infrangibility of the ceremony they had gone through.

"When do they come?" asked Emma.

"In an hour or so."

"I shall come in and listen to what goes on."

"I think you had better not, Nem, dear. There—there is likely—perhaps there might be a struggle with some of the prisoners, and——"

"What matter? Goodness me, Denzil, you're positively becoming imbecile! You have talked the most outrageous nonsense for the last five minutes. You have spoken of the arrest of some smugglers as if your dearest friends were about to be hanged. You have paid me the compliment to acknowledge that "we were man and wife—yes, yes, of course," with a lugubrious countenance, and now you are for thinking that I am in danger of a handful of scamps who are hand-bound and delivered over into military custody."

Denzil was in no humour for banter; he struck his forehead with his hand, and strode up and down the room.

"Why you're not angry with me for laughing at you?" asked Emma, coming up to him, and laying her hand on his arm. He turned upon her fiercely, and positively took her by the throat somewhat roughly. She was frightened, and he saw it, and seemed ill at ease himself.

"That is what some one did to me in the darkness of last night—twice!" It was true Denzil had imagined this at the time, but I fancy, in saying so, he rather found an excuse for his violence now, than acted as he had done to illustrate what he said.

"Why, Denzil, what *is* the matter with you to-day? You must be ill, you are so strange."

"Forgive me, Nem; I am harassed to death!" So he stooped to kiss her, and then adding, "I must go and make preparations for Trenbrase," left the room.

She looked after him in wonder. She had never seen him so strange. The more she thought over the brief interview, the more anxious she became about him.

"It is quite clear," she thought to herself, "I must attend in the justice hall to see how he behaves. I verily believe he is suffering from a twinge of conscience. Dear me! I wonder what conscience is like."

So saying, she sat down at the harpsicord again, and ran her fingers over the keys.

> "And I'll stand as true to my true love,
> As the stars stand true in the sky,"

she sang, and her clear sweet voice went ringing out through the open window, and Denzil heard it as he crossed the garden to the lodge. And he knit his brows as if some sudden pain had smitten him.

It was not very long before Lord Trenbrase arrived. The news of Aubyn's disinherison had not yet reached him, so Denzil had the unpleasant task of telling his lordship all about it. To do Trenbrase justice, he was blunt and honest enough. But had he been a little more courteous it would have been well.

"Humph!" said he, "sorry for it, sorry for it. Good young fellow; would have done credit to Tresellan."

All of which, as I daresay he himself felt ten minutes (not less) after he had said it, was rather a one-sided compliment to Denzil.

"Well, Sir Denzil, so these rascals are taken red-hand, eh?" he inquired, as if he wished to turn the subject. "Red-hand—with laces, and silks, and wine, and brandy, and tobacco stowed about them?"

"I cannot say,—I have heard no more than you lordship."

"Faith, that's nothing at all. But there is one thing I should like to hear."

"What is it?" asked Denzil.

"Why, I should like to hear you order a stoup of claret, for my ride here has parched my throat like a blacksmith's chimney."

No sooner said than done. In another minute or so his lordship was as comfortable as he ever was in this world of care, dipping his nose in the wine.

Presently arose a great trampling of feet, and the officer at the head of his company marched into Tresellan gates, followed by all the gaping community of Polvadnick. It was utterly in vain that the porter essayed to keep the curious out of the grounds.

He locked the gate, but the crowd filtered through the hedges and over the palings. At last, in despair, he flung the gates open, thinking, perhaps, they would do less harm by entering in the legitimate manner than by forcing their way elsewhere.

Picture the astonishment and awe of Denzil and Emma when they saw Christopher escorted between two of the soldiers!

The lawyer had spent a troubled night; he was looking pale, and his usually rosy gills were flaccid and white. He looked at Denzil, however, with confidence, for he felt sure that in him he had a tower of defence. Denzil was coming forward to meet him, but a frown from the lawyer checked him. Christopher thought, and rightly, that Denzil could aid him best by seeming not to advocate his cause for friendship, but for justice and equity.

The sailors of the lugger, about eighteen in number, were as ill-looking a crew as you might see in a year's sail. They were a mixture of French, Dutch, and English, and about as hang-dog a batch of specimens of those nations as the Newgate Calendar could wish. They were ranged against the wall between two guards, with loaded firelocks.

Lord Trenbrase sat at the head of the table, the officer on his right, Denzil on his left, while Emma drew her chair close behind her husband's. A crowd of the Polvadnick washed, and unwashed, crowded the end of the hall, being kept back by half a dozen marines.

It was an immense relief to Denzil to see that Martha was not present among the prisoners. He looked in wonder at Christopher, who understood the meaning of the glance, but was quite as much at a loss as Denzil.

In front of the crowd stood little Kit, and very uncomfortable he looked and felt. I believe he was much troubled in mind to find himself assisting that Law of which he had always hitherto taken such pains to transgress the provisions. He stood swaying in an uncouth manner first on one leg and then on the other, and by no means encouraged by the hortatory whispers of Zachariah Vercoe. That worthy having hitherto been connected in the lad's mind with canings and threats, it seemed to be a subversion of the natural order of things for him to be whispering, "Be bould, manny; speak up the truth, the whole truth, and nothing but the truth. Thee'rt a brave child; never fear, manny!"

How did Pentowan feel? Well, anxious, uncomfortable, certainly, but tolerably confident as to the result. He felt sure that he had enough hold on Denzil to make him exert himself to the utmost to keep him from danger. Nevertheless he felt that his character was irretrievably gone, though he hoped, by sheer dint of perjury, to upset the boy's evidence; how, he was not exactly prepared to say, but that was the line of defence he had set up for himself.

At the suggestion of the officer, the crew of the lugger were disposed of first. Of course, as they were taken *in flagrante delicto*, there was no room to doubt their guilt, and Lord Trenbrase committed them without scruple. Moreover, he read them a serious lecture on the awful nature of their crime, a discourse which might have had more weight if it had not been pretty generally believed that much of the spirit which had tinged his lordship's jovial countenance had never passed through the hands of a custom-house officer.

Then came Pentowan's turn. The boy was examined very closely by Lord Trenbrase, for he had long known Christopher, and was rather loth to believe—not so much that he was guilty of having to do with illicit cargoes, as that he could be proved to be so. But the lad's testimony was not easily shaken. Denzil, with Trenbrase's permission, also examined the boy, and Pentowan put him under a cross-examination of the most searching kind. Christopher had not been a rogue and a "rogue's lawyer" so many years without having learnt how to cross-examine; but the boy answered fairly all that was asked of him, and the testimony he gave remained unshaken.

But at last Christopher hit on a method by which to throw doubt on the evidence. He had been permitted to sit at the table, and was supplied with paper. On a little scrap he wrote a question, and crumpling it up in his hand unseen, managed, by reaching over, ostensibly to get a book, to deposit it by Denzil, whose attention he drew to it afterwards. Denzil took up the slip,—and the cue. Turning to Kit, he asked—

"I see you have the mark of a blow across your face—how did you come by it?"

"He did it," said the boy, casting a revengeful look at Christopher, who immediately broke in.

"The boy, my lord, was pestering me and hanging about my house, and, I regret to say, in a moment of anger I struck at him, and unintentionally hit him across the face instead of the shoulders."

Trenbrase gave a long whistle. Like most shallow people, he fancied himself remarkably acute. He at once saw exactly what Pentowan had intended he should—malice and revenge as the promptings of the accusation, and he was mightily charmed with his own penetration.

"Did he utter any threat, or make use of any expression which might be construed into an intention to be revenged?" he asked of the lawyer.

"He did, my lord, though I gave no particular heed at the time, and therefore cannot undertake to repeat his words."

"Clear enough!" remarked Lord Trenbrase in a sort of aside to Denzil. "Malice—malice—vindictive malice, eh!"

"I have no doubt you are right!"

Christopher ventured a bold step.

"Of course it would be of no use for me to swear; but these sailors here, whom I *could* swear

I had never seen, would, I have no doubt, say if they know me?"

The smugglers knew their own fate sealed for the present, and felt that it was for their own future safety that Pentowan should go free. Under such circumstances, of course a little perjury was "no object" to such unscrupulous gentry, so they moodily stared at Christopher and shook their heads, one of the men adding, moreover, that "he knew him by sight, for he (the sailor) was Polvadnick born, but he knew the lawyer had nought to do with the 'Flying Spray.'"

"I think, under the circumstances," Trenbrase appealed to Denzil, "there is nothing more to be said. We must discharge Mr. Pentowan."

"Without a stain on his character," interjected Denzil.

"And retain the boy in custody."

Things were going very unpleasantly for poor Kit, you see; but he seemed to be not much alarmed, for the officer was looking and nodding at him encouragingly. He had hitherto taken no part in the proceedings, but now he rose, and motioning to two of his men to stand on either side of Christopher, who was preparing to beat a precipitate retreat by way of victory, he turned to Lord Trenbrase.

"With your permission, my lord, I have some more evidence of this prisoner's connection with the smuggling vessel; but there is another charge to be brought against him. Speak up, boy; what is it you charge this man with?"

"I charge him," said Kit, very distinctly and boldly, "with the murder of Sir Abel Tresellan."

If a thunderbolt had fallen into the centre of the table round which they were sitting, Trenbrase, Denzil, Pentowan, and Emma could not have been more startled.

CHAPTER XXVII.

THE STORM THICKENS.

It was true! The rosy round face that glanced down the barrel which conveyed the missive of death to poor Sir Abel. was the same one that now, white, bloodless, quivering, devoured with its eyes the countenances of Denzil and Emma.

Before the tumult which this statement had excited was subsiding, a woman pressed forward from the crowd, and pushing by the marines, came up to Kit. It was Martha. Throwing one arm round the boy's neck, she pointed at Christopher, and with a triumphant laugh cried out—

"Ha, ha! loving parents make fond children. The boy has put the halter round his own father's neck!"

"Good Heavens!" exclaimed Trenbrase, "is that imp the lawyer's son?"

"Ay, that is he!" said Martha, "though they neither knew of their relationship till now. That boy is the son of Christopher Pentowan, who betrayed the mother and deserted the babe.

That white-faced rogue—that black-hearted villain, whose whole life has been one long crime—he is the father of this poor boy, that he has so cruelly ill-treated. Years ago, my Lord Trenbrase, I have seen you, and fitted your hand with gloves."

"Egad, I remember your face now! Why, you are Mistress Martha, the mercer's pretty wife!" said Trenbrase.

"Listen!" said Martha. "Years ago, when I used to sell your lordship gloves and hose, that man there had an honest, but unfortunate man for a client. While he was at his client's house one day, he saw the wife, and plotted her ruin. She was a fool—she believed he loved her—she left her husband, and fled with the lawyer. Rather more than a year after her leaving her husband's roof, she gave birth to a child. By that time that man had wearied of her, and he deserted her. She was too proud to pursue him, too poor to punish him. She struggled on with the child for a time, but the child grew daily more and more like in her eyes to the wretch who had ruined her. She was not rich in love for anything; she had hate, and to spare. She deserted the child at the door of a fisherman's cottage in Polvadnick. The child was adopted by the poor people, and grew up a little wild beast—as what else should it be? And when the fisherman died it lived like a wild beast, and this is the child!"

"And the mother?" asked Trenbrase.

"I am his mother!"

"You!" exclaimed Denzil, whose prudence forsook him entirely, so utterly overwhelmed was he by the strange wild story he had just heard.

"You his mother!" he repeated.

"Yes, fool, I was deceived by him years before I was deceived by you!"

At this you may guess Emma fired up.

"What do you mean, woman? Denzil, what does this drab mean? What has there been between you and her? Speak! and silence her shrewish, slanderous tongue."

"Oh! oh! so you can spit fire, you wax doll," cried Martha, stung by Emma's words. Our fair witch had looked so tiny and quiet that the elder woman was not quite prepared to be attacked by her. "Drab, in your teeth, how dare *you* stand there by my husband, and lay your hand on his arm?"

There was no mistaking whom she claimed as her husband, for there stood Emma grasping Denzil savagely by the wrist as she spoke, trying to rouse him from the state of stupefaction into which he had fallen.

She dropt his arm as if it had been an adder at Martha's last words. She looked in Denzil's face, and saw that what she said was true. If it was possible that anything could have atoned for the evil Emma had done, it would have been the overpowering agony that tortured and distracted her at this moment. I think even Aubyn, whom she had so deeply wronged, would have pitied and forgiven her if he could have seen her now.

She fell back into a chair and gasped for breath.

Everybody was gasping for breath, you may well imagine. There stood Martha in the midst, her bosom heaving, her eyes flashing, and all around her were awe-struck and dumb. It was as if some great serpent were coiled in the midst exerting a fearful fascination over them.

Lord Trenbrase was the first to recover himself.

"By George," he murmured, "things are coming to a head now—egad, smuggling's a gnat-bite to this—murder and bigamy! Why, captain, what's to be done next?"

The captain was inclined to doubt the truth of Martha's story—or at all events to believe that

Denzil had only entrapped her into a false marriage. But a few minutes sufficed to clear up all question on that score. From a small silk bag hung round her neck and thrust into the bosom of her gown Martha produced her "marriage lines." She had placed them, with a lock of Denzil's hair and one or two other little relics in that receptacle before going on board the lugger; for not being quite certain what might turn up, she wisely determined to carry all her valuables about her person.

Denzil meanwhile sat with his head buried in his arms, and bowed upon the table. Emma was fairly broken down, and was weeping bitterly. As for Pentowan, next to his terror about himself, I think he was positively indulging in a little delight at the view of such an amount of iniquity and remorse. In fact he felt that he was not alone in the mire.

The officer was the most self-possessed of the party. He knew nothing of any of the persons concerned, and only cared to see justice administered. He took Christopher more particularly under his care, as the "prize of his shield and spear." It was with a view to putting his guilt beyond a doubt that he called Kit to him.

"Were any of these men here," he pointed

to the smugglers, "on board the boat when the prisoner fired at Sir Abel?"

"About half of 'em, I should say," was the answer.

"Look here, my men!" said the captain, turning to the row of sailors, "you have been found guilty of smuggling; but this question of murder is a much more serious matter. I have no hesitation in saying that those among you who will give evidence about that, will not be heavily punished for the contraband business."

"Honour among thieves" is of all proverbs (and they are as a rule false) the most erroneous that ever was invented. It is curious to see in the police reports how, almost to a certainty, when a gang of burglars or pickpockets have been performing some feat of dexterity, the first man caught at once delivers up his "pals." When Inspector Whicher tells Bill Sykes he is wanted for that little plate job down the river, William almost invariably says, "Why don't you take the Artful Dodger, he was as much in as I was." And the Artful Dodger in his turn suggests some one else, and so on, until the Inspector is able to tell the magistrate how, "from information he received," he took up the prisoners on the charge of burglariously breaking into a house and stealing therefrom a quantity of plate. "Honour among thieves!" why it's absurd on the face of it. What a very inconvenient thing it would be! A certain sort of professional etiquette there may be among lawyers, but honour among thieves—why it's ridiculous!

The captain had counted on this characteristic of roguery, and so he was quite prepared to see two or three of the men stand forward and declare themselves ready to depose to the truth of the boy's story. As one of them said, too, "Running a cargo is one thing, and a fair stand-up fight with the coast-guard, but shooting a man in cold blood wasn't in their way of business—and he was glad the murder was out."

You will now have the goodness to look at the state of affairs carefully, for there is some complication. There is Sir Denzil Tresellan guilty of bigamy. There is Christopher Pentowan accused of murder by his own son. There is Emma a wife, yet not a wife, and Martha the rightful claimant to the title of Lady Tresellan.

What was to be done? Trenbrase consulted with the captain. The captain was certain on one point—that Christopher should be taken to the lock-up at the Town Hall. As regarded Denzil, he was inclined to suggest that he should "consider himself under arrest"—a military procedure which Trenbrase did not think applicable.

But in the midst of the confusion which the events of the last quarter of an hour had created, there was a sudden cry of "Here comes Mr. Aubyn!" "Make way for Mr. Aubyn!" cried Trenbrase, delighted at the notion of getting his cool judgment to assist him.

So Aubyn made his way up to the table. He looked around him in some surprise, for he of course was quite ignorant of what had occurred, and had yet to learn his brother's double marriage, and the name of his father's murderer.

But Aubyn, I must tell you, did not come alone.

CHAPTER XXVIII.

THE ELUCIDATION OF MYSTERIES.

I must, in order to explain Aubyn's appearance at Tresellan, take you back to the night of the capture of the "Spray."

You remember how Lucinda revealed to Aubyn what a cruel plot had been contrived to deprive him of his birthright. Stung to the heart by such wickedness and heartlessness in those whom he had long loved and cherished, he was driven almost to frenzy.

He was, besides, penniless, and possessed no means of obtaining money.

These two things must be his excuse for the course which he adopted.

You will recollect his vow to become an Ishmael with his hand against every man's. The thought which gave rise to that utterance was the thought of taking to the road.

I avow it is not a nice thing to have to confess to one's readers that the hero of this novel turned highwayman. But the profession in the days of George II. was by no means looked upon as entirely ungentlemanly. In fact it was held as a sort of chivalry—a knight-errantry, which people smiled upon, or only frowned at when they had their own pockets lightened.

Ladies visited the knights of the black vizor in prison, and wept over and made love to them. Artists and painters made calls on them, and noblemen and gentlemen did not scorn to associate with them in their last days. They went to death gaily, dressed in purple and fine linen, and took a farewell bowl and pledged a parting toast on their way to Tyburn, amid the tears and mournful admiration of a large and highly respectable—nay, even noble—audience.

Shades of Hind, Holloway, Duval, and Turpin! must I make excuses for the pursuit in which you delighted, and the profession you adorned? I will do nothing of the kind; so here goes without any more preamble. I "stand, and deliver" myself of the statement that Aubyn, on the night of which I am speaking, rode out of Polvadnick on to the moors towards Saltash, and wore a crape over his face, and carried his pistols in his coat pocket.

Now it so happened that not being an experienced knight of the road, he neglected to examine these pistols as closely as an old hand would have done. He, in fact, contented himself with putting some fresh priming in their pans, and took it for granted that the bullets, with which he had loaded them on the night previous, were still there.

The moon was hidden at intervals by the flying clouds as Aubyn reached the heath. The first thing he did was one which betrayed, as clearly as the neglect to examine his pistols, what an inexperienced workman he was. He set spurs to his horse, and galloped as if for bare life round and round the race-course, as it was still called, though there had not been races there since Charles the Second's time, when Lord Trenbrase's ancestor had kept a stud.

I fancy this unwise act was a sort of safety-valve. The motion of the horse, and the cool night air on his forehead, roused yet calmed him. He shook off his gloom and despair for a stern and fixed resolve to avenge himself on mankind for the wrong his brother had done him,—to make the world at large reimburse him for the loss of his inheritance. He pulled up his panting steed in the shadow of two or three stunted trees that had taken possession of a knoll of ground not a stone's throw from the high road. He had not been waiting long before he heard the sound of hoofs in the distance. Nearer and nearer in the silence of the night they came, and presently he began to make out a single horseman approaching through the mist that lay breast-high over the waste. It would have occurred to a regular highwayman that this was a brother of the road perhaps. But Aubyn never thought of that—as the traveller came up abreast the trees, he galloped out and called on him to stop. Had he been up to his work he would have started out earlier, so as to come abreast of the stranger—as it was, the latter put spurs to his horse, and by the time Aubyn had reached the road had got a good start ahead. But Aubyn's horse, winded though it was by the gallop it had had, was better than the traveller's sorry nag. A few strides carried our hero alongside. Twice he called on the traveller to halt—and then he fired. To do him credit he aimed at the horse's shoulder. Of course, thanks to Lucinda's precautions, the result was merely a flash, bright enough to display the horsemen's faces to each other—for Aubyn's hat and crape had blown off in the pursuit.

"Mr. Aubyn! Good heavens, what is the meaning of this?"

"Mr. Williams—where on earth do you drop from?"

Yes! It was Gregory. And a long story he had to tell, as he and Aubyn (who first, however, recovered his hat, though not without some search) rode slowly down toward Polvadnick.

Aubyn had learnt from Lucinda that Pentowan had seen Gregory killed by robbers in Italy, so Gregory had to explain how Pentowan's misapprehension arose. It seems that thanks to his stumbling down stairs, and being actually falling at the time when he was struck, the old clerk escaped what would otherwise inevitably have been a death-blow. As it was he was stunned, and lay insensible, until long after the inn had been fired. He was found eventually by some goatherds, who had been attracted to the spot by the flames. By them he was restored to consciousness, and carried to their huts before the Sbirri arrived at the scene of the conflagration. Their rude medicine was speedily put into requisition, and in a shorter time possibly than it would have taken had he fallen into a regular doctor's hands, his wound was in a fair way to heal. As soon as he had sufficiently recovered to be able to stir, he set out without delay for England.

"And here I am, sir," he concluded; "and here, sir, are the documents which Mr. Rewth went to fetch!" So saying he placed a sealed packet in Aubyn's hands.

"Why, how in heaven's name! did you get possession of these?"

"Well, Mr. Aubyn, it's a longish story; first of all Mr. Pentowan tried to get them from the priest, and would have got them too, but Mr. Frank just reached there in time. Well, the priest died, and we set out together to a place that I forget the name of. There, while I was nodding over the fire, and when Mr. Frank was rather overcome with wine, my master got him to bring out the packet. Presently Mr. Frank dropt asleep, and lo and behold, Mr. Pentowan all of a sudden picked it up and pitched it slap into the fire at my feet. For a second or so I did not know what to do. Luckily somebody came to the door just then, and while my master's attention was taken off the fire I picked the packet out. It was just a bit scorched, and in a moment more would have been a-light."

"But did not Pentowan look round again?"

"Ah, of course, sir! But"—and here the old man's voice began to falter—"I put some other papers in the fire in the place of the packet.

They were my mother's letters, Mr. Aubyn. My father died when I was a baby, and my mother reared me and taught me, for she was very poor; and when I came to Polvadnick she used to write to me, and she's been dead these thirty years now, and I'd kept all her letters since. But I knew that if she could have seen what I did she'd have approved of it, for she always taught me to be honest and just, and to do right at any cost. And, oh dear, Mr. Aubyn, now that I see what he's like—what a deal of wrong I have done at my master's orders!"

It was late at night when Aubyn and Gregory reached the "Ship,"—for Aubyn determined to quit the lawyer's roof for ever. They sat up till nearly daybreak, for Gregory had to tell Aubyn of all that had taken place at Terini and Mentazza in detail.

Then they opened the packet, and Aubyn was delighted to find the necessary evidence of his father's marriage drawn up in due form by Sir Abel's own hand, together with a statement by Father Seraphicus explaining the history of the whole matter.

So now, if you please, we will return to the justice room at Tresellan.

Aubyn walked up to the table, placed the

documents before Lord Trenbrase, and said, "I, Aubyn Tresellan, the lawful son of Sir Abel, claim this house and seigniory, to which these papers show my title!"

To the astonishment of everybody a laugh—a loud wild laugh—rang through the room.

It came from Denzil; he rose with a flushed face and glittering eye.

"A Tresellan!" he shouted. "A Tresellan! come, sea-dogs, and eat your brothers!"

He was mad! The hereditary malady had been awakened by the fierce conflict of fear, shame, and remorse that had wrung his bosom. The words were doubtless prompted by a recollection of the family tradition which he had so often heard as a child.

CHAPTER XXIX.

THE FALL OF THE CURTAIN.

EVERYBODY's getting up and preparing to go; opera cloaks are being "helped on," great coats are struggled into, playbills are crumpled up and thrown under foot. The play is not quite ended, but everybody knows now what is to finish it. Only a few resolute sight-seers sit and watch the joining of hands, and listen to the tag.

I suppose novel-readers are like play-goers, so I will not detain you now. I'm going to put the canvas over the boxes, and draw up the chandelier.

Nevertheless, as some persistent readers may like to see the final group and hear the last words of my story, I will briefly tell the fate of my poor players, who have strutted and fretted their hour upon the stage.

Christopher Pentowan was removed to the lock-up. The next morning the sentry saw him apparently gazing out at the window with his head a little on one side, as if he were criticising the face of nature. But the face of nature had no more interest for this critic—he had committed suicide by hanging himself from the bars of the casement.

Denzil was hopelessly insane. At the little cottage on the Perl he lingered for years, a raving, gibbering madman. But he was not left only to the care of hirelings. A pale, ghostly, thin-looking woman, with fair hair and blue eyes, watched and tended him to the last. The girl, who perilled her soul for him, whom he deceived and wronged, clung to him until the last. It was her hand that smoothed his burning forehead, that closed his dying eyes. The love which was born in crime was purified in trial,—and she "loved much."

Of Martha I know nothing certain, but from the old letters and memoranda, of which I have spoken as my sources of information touching the Tresellan history, I gather materials for surmise. I am inclined to think that she went away to France with her son Kit. He, having rescued Bowser and made his peace with him, was taken into partnership in a fresh smuggling speculation, which eventually became quite as flourishing as that on which that luckless lugger, the "Flying Spray" was employed.

Aubyn and Lucinda, I need scarcely tell you, were married, though not until some three years after the events I have described. The reason of the delay is to be found in Lucinda's horror lest Aubyn should ever repent of having married the daughter of his father's murderer. It was long ere he could overcome her scruples. But at last she gave her consent, and they were married. And on his death-bed Aubyn could turn his eyes on the mother of his children and say with truth that he had never for one moment regretted that he had taken to wife his first love, Lucinda Pentowan.

Gregory lived at Tresellan for the rest of his time. The poor old man never completely recovered from that blow on the head which had so nearly brought this history to a different conclusion.

The curtain descends, the play is played out, the lamps are turned down.

As I sit here in the gray twilight of approaching morning I hear the rain dripping from the eaves without, and the sea sighing under the Tresellan cliffs.

I lay the yellow worn old letters I have had such trouble to decipher, on the red embers of the wood fire, and watch the flame creep up and consume them.

It dies out; and the sparks in the black tinkling heap go out and in, and run, and spread, and die away.

And as the wind that ushers in the morning sweeps over the sea it comes through the tower where Old Morse is hanging; and I can hear that the ancient bell has swayed in that mysterious breath of the day. One solemn low muffled stroke shudders past upon the air, and dies away into silence.

It tolls the knell of those last records of the Tresellans of Tresellan.

THE END.

CPSIA information can be obtained
at www.ICGtesting.com
Printed in the USA
LVHW040340110522
718423LV00001B/286

9 783375 007263